PROJECT VALHALLA

AN OMNILOGOS SINGULARITY NOVELLA

MICHELE AMITRANI

ISBN (eBook): 978-1-988770-53-6

ISBN (Paperback): 978-1-988770-58-1

First Edition 2023

Published by Michele Amitrani.

Cover Design by 100 Covers

AUTHOR'S NOTE

Project Valhalla takes place between the books *Rise of Polaris* and *Legacy of Ariul*, the first and the second book in The Omnilogos Singularity series.

To avoid spoilers I suggest you read the first book, before diving into this novella.

Happy reading!

Michele

PART I

VALHALLA

1

INTERLOOP

(2023)

"I've put two years of my life into this project, Ben. You can't do this."

The man sitting behind the desk spread his hands on the leather ledger in front of him. "Look, it's been a tough year for the Institute, Selene. The board of directors strangled our funds. I'm sorry. We need to pick what's going to sell. I can't afford to use what we've got left for anything we'd like."

"*Anything*?" Selene walked up to him, hands shaking. "*This* is the Institute's flagship project you're talking about."

"*Was.*" Ben's voice was calm, soothing even. "The council wants to focus on projects with practical applications. I can't argue with that. It's their money we're spending."

Selene narrowed her eyes. "Interloop is the most practical project in the goddamn world!"

"Not for them, it's not. They think that moving objects via interlink isn't exactly the best use of their funds."

"And what do *you* think?"

"Doesn't matter. The money isn't mine."

"I asked you a question."

Ben shrugged. "Okay. Interloop has potential, but it needs a lot more time, funding, and attention than the Institute can give it. You've proven this in the past few months." He picked up the ledger, opened it, and started reading. "Two interconnected control stations, a phase detector for energy exchanges, intrasynaptic occurrence plates... Do I need to keep going? You have any idea how much this costs?"

Selene slammed her hands on the desk. "You have the money. You're just deciding not to use it for Interloop. At least have the decency to answer my question."

Ben sighed. He ran a hand over his head. "Do you really want me to spell it out to you?"

Selene opened her arms. "Hit me."

"Okay." Ben leaned forward, looking at her with eyes so brown they seemed black. "Selene Sato, you are the most brilliant person I know. This Institute owes you awards, recognition, and prestige. I have no problem admitting that."

"But?"

"But you're also a pain in the ass, and see only what's in front of your nose."

"What the hell is that supposed to mean?"

"It means that Interloop is a projection of your blindness. It doesn't matter how brilliant it is if no one can put a price tag on it and sell it to the highest bidder."

"What are you talking about? I sent a detailed analysis of the—"

"It's not enough," Ben cut her off. "You gave the board a couple reports and some useless statistics. These aren't things that can pay the bills. We're no charity, for Christ's sake. We need rock-solid results and—"

"Look, if I just had a little more time—"

"No." Ben almost shouted the word. "It's over. Interloop is dead. End of story."

"I—"

"But there's good news."

"Good news? What good news?"

"The archons have assigned you to the Samjon calibrator, the one Professor Woming is working on."

"What?" Selene barked a laugh. "Please tell me you're joking."

"What's the problem?"

"The Samjon? A monkey with a goddamn wrench could take care of that."

"It already has a buyer. It's more than you can say for Interloop."

"You'll get twenty, maybe thirty thousand dollars." Selene waved a hand dismissively. "Pittance compared to Interloop's potentials."

"Did I stutter? Interloop is over, Selene. Make peace with the decision and move on."

Selene clenched her jaw. "Tell me, Ben Reno Somoza, when was the last time you looked at a project not for its price tag, but for the difference it could make for the entire human race?"

"Poetic speeches won't pay your mortgage."

"What?" Selene's frown was deep. "What's that supposed to mean?"

"I know you bought a new apartment." Ben crossed his arms as he looked at her. "Devin told me. Are you paying for that with wishful thinking? Hmm? Bet you need hard cash for that one."

Selene recoiled as if someone had slapped her. "That's none of your goddamned business."

"Really? Maybe it's not. It doesn't matter. What matters is

that you can't be squeamish. It wasn't easy convincing the archons not to give you the boot."

"Oh. Really? You want me to kiss your ass? You think screwing up two years' worth of work and relegating me to the Institute's dungeon to tighten screws makes you my savior?"

"Settle down, Selene. It's over. At least for now. Look, I'll tell you what. Why don't we wait till next year? By that time, the board might have enough funding for—"

"Hell no." Selene could feel her heart slamming against her chest. "Don't fucking insult my intelligence. You can sell that bullshit speech to a first-year grad who hasn't been around the block and knows shit about how projects die. If you cut Interloop now, it's over forever."

"I'm just trying to meet you in the middle."

"Really? You're doing a shitty job at that." She turned and stalked toward the office's door.

"Selene—"

"Tomorrow," she cut him off, her hand on the door handle, "when you receive my letter of resignation, sign it knowing that you've turned down this Institute's greatest chance of going down in the history books."

"You're making a poor decision and you know it. Why don't you—"

"A poor decision was sticking around in this place for two years," Selene cut him off. "Now *this* is the best choice I've made in a long time." She gave Ben the middle finger, then slammed the door and stormed out of the building.

2

POSSIBILITIES

(2024)

A year of failures.

Four words with which Selene could sum up the moment she had quit working for the Evan Den Bawer Institute to go look for investors by herself until now.

She had tried to sell Interloop's technology to research centers, universities, start-ups, government agencies, and wealthy individuals.

Everyone had shown interest in her flashy presentations, but when it came to writing the six-figure check she needed to continue her research, they had disappeared faster than a politician at the end of an election campaign.

A lot had changed after she'd slammed the door in Ben's face to go her own way.

For starters, she'd had to sell her apartment and move into the suburbs, where she now shared a half-century-old basement with two students half her age.

Her bank account was overdrawn, weighed down by a credit card debt so massive, she wasn't sure one lifetime would be enough to pay it off.

What else? The last three job interviews had gone south faster than an airline charter hit by a missile. She'd sent her resume to dozens of institutions across the States, but apparently at the moment researchers and faculty members were as common as sand in the desert. Nobody needed her.

She had reached the bottom long ago, now she was scraping her way down to hell.

Selene entered the shithole she called home, tossed her purse on the kitchen counter, and sank on the brown couch that a thousand years before might have been red.

She rubbed her wrists with a groan and put her legs on the footrest. Her part-time job was killing her. The coffee shop at Denven and Suarez Street was supposed to be a temporary fallback, something to keep her afloat while she was looking for a real job.

What she thought would be a few days' gig turned into a month, then two months. Well, the months added up pretty quickly. She'd been wearing the expresso-stained, cinnamon-smelly maroon apron for six months.

Selene pushed herself up from the couch and hit the bathroom.

She took a long, hot shower and finished just in time to feel hungry. She took a slice of Margherita pizza from the fridge—a leftover from the day before. Or was it *two* days before? The bread crust was stale, but she had survived worse things. She put the pizza in the microwave and set the timer.

While she was waiting for her dinner, she grabbed her cellphone and checked her inbox.

"Awesome. More good news." She went through her messages quickly, scanning the content and then moving on to the next message. None of the research centers in the Midwest cared for her hands-on demonstration of Interloop, and only one of the five universities she'd contacted to send a job application responded by declining her offer. Right. Another slap in the face. If she'd had a dime every time she got a *no*, she'd be a freaking millionaire by now.

"What the hell..." Selene noticed the smoke a second after she smelled the awful stench of her dinner burning.

"Fuck!" She ran to the microwave, turned it off, and opened the microwave door. A thick cloud of smoke wafted through the basement and Selene coughed. She opened the only window in the apartment and spent the next fifteen minutes trying to get rid of the smoke.

When the air became breathable again, she dumped what was left of her dinner in the garbage bin and took the last can of tuna from the bottom shelf of the kitchen.

An hour later, she was staring at a bottle of Marqués de Riscal. She had placed it on the highest shelf, stripped the label, and substituted it with another from an apple vinegar bottle. It worked to prevent her roommates from thinking that it was okay to take a sip or two. It was cheap wine, but it was wine. It was supposed to be her way to celebrate good news. A new job, funding for her project, finding five bucks on the street. *Any* good news, really.

She waited months for that news, and the world had just laughed in her face.

"Whatever." She raised her left hand toward the bottle on the shelf, and the bottle vibrated. "Come on. Come to mama."

The bottle lifted a few inches from the shelf and then swayed dangerously for a moment before traveling the distance to Selene.

When it was in her hand, she opened the cork and poured the contents into a glass.

She stared at the hyperonic chip attached to the label.

That thin layer of carbonduren made that magic happen. The chip functioned as a proxy for the Interloop's device she had implanted under her skin. Whenever she connected her interlink to the chip's infrawaves, she could control the object's movement, like she just had.

Her ex-colleagues at the Evan Den Bawer Institute called it the "six-figure sinkhole." None of them believed it was worth their attention.

They missed the bigger picture.

Moving objects from a distance was just one of the applications of Interloop. It was true Selene had never done more than impress people with her technology, but it had the potential to change entire industries.

She just hadn't had the skill set to convince people of it.

Selene was staring at a half-empty wine bottle before she knew it.

"Time to cut your losses." Selene moved her hand idly, making the bottle sway gently on top of the table. "Close the bottle and go to bed. Doctor's orders."

But she didn't. She just couldn't bring herself to stand from that chair and go to bed.

All that waited for her in the bedroom was another sleepless night. And after that, the height of the day: six hours spent smiling at strangers while serving them cheese-cakes and almond milk lattes.

Fuck that.

The bottle hit the table and almost fell on the ground. She had to reach out and grasp it at the last second.

"Shit." She ran a shaky hand over her hair. The interlink connection stopped working at random times. It was a problem she had never had the time to fix.

Selene breathed out slowly, closing the wine bottle and staring at it with glassy eyes.

Who was she kidding? It was all her fault. Walking away from Ben's office was the first mistake she made. The second had been believing she could sell her project.

How could she be so stupid? She had no background in marketing, no way of knowing what to do to sell her idea, and no one to help her. She was a researcher with a résumé as long as the Great Wall of China, but zero idea what to do with it.

She wanted investors to shell out piles of cash for an invention that was barely more reliable than the microwave that roasted her dinner.

What the hell was she thinking?

Ben was right. Selene was reckless, blind to her own foolishness. She'd let her emotions get in the way, and now she was paying the price. She should have kept her mouth shut and—

Her cellphone vibrated. Selene picked it from her pocket and read the message.

I'm waiting outside your house. Bring the bottle of wine with you when you come out.

Selene blinked. She read the message again, then checked the sender.

Unknown number.

Might have been a mistake? But the message said something about a bottle of wine.

Selene went to check out the window. The street looked empty.

She bit her lip. Her fingers moved across the display.

Who are you?

She sent the message and waited.

No answer. Again, she checked outside.

Selene's mind was working slowly; the wine was already getting to her head.

Part of her wanted to sit back, forget about the message, and finish the contents of the bottle. The other part wanted to figure out who sent that message.

Before weariness got the better of her, she grabbed her coat and walked out of the basement, taking the bottle with her.

∽

IT WAS RAINING. Not a heavy, angry rain, lashing at the concrete sidewalk of Scion Street; just a lazy, barely notice-able drip of water.

Selene looked around, frowning. The street continued to appear empty. The broken streetlight certainly didn't help her see in the dark, but there was enough light coming from the apartments nearby to see around.

Selene checked her phone again, thinking she might have missed something.

"Do you need someone's help to finish the other half?"

Selene turned sharply toward the voice. A figure wrapped in a heavy dark coat was leaning against the broken light pole.

"What?" Selene stepped backward, surprised by the sudden appearance.

"The wine." The stranger pointed to the bottle. "I've heard it's bad luck to drink a whole bottle by yourself."

"Did you write the message?"

"I would have come in, but I figure we'll have more room for your demonstration here, outside."

"Demonstration?" Selene tried to ignore the throbbing in her temples. "What are you talking about?"

"I'm talking about the moment you try to convince me to fund your project."

"To fund my..." Selene trailed off. She narrowed her eyes at the stranger. He was a very short fellow with shaggy hair and almond-shaped eyes. He looked little more than a teenager. "Who the hell are you?"

"My name's Wei." He glanced at the bottle, smirking. "I saw your little magic trick back there." He nodded toward the open window of her basement. "It was impressive. I'd like to see it again."

"What's this? A prank?" Selene squinted her eyes, trying to push back the fogginess in her mind. Damned wine. When she spoke again, her voice was slurred. "Who sent you? Ben? Devin? What the fuck do you want from me?"

"Get a grip, Doctor. I'm good news. In fact, I'm the one person you've been dying to meet for the past year. Now, you wanted a chance to show Interloop to someone who would get it. I'm here. Show me."

"Yeah? Really?" Selene threw the bottle on the ground. It shattered in a dozen pieces. "I'm not falling for it, asshole. You hear me? Fuck them and their fucking Institute!"

The young man shook his head. "What a waste." He picked up the shards of glass, tossing them into a garbage bin. "I see you're not in the mood for a chat. All right. It might be my fault. I should have picked a better time to talk, but when I found out about Interloop, I couldn't believe it. I wanted to see it for myself."

Selene snorted. "You think I'm an idiot? How old are you? Fifteen? Sixteen? You expect me to believe this bull-shit? You're not even..."

Her cellphone chirped.

"Read the message." Wei crossed his arms. "Might be important."

Selene pulled her cell phone out. Someone had just sent

a money transfer into her bank account. She read the amount and nearly blacked out.

"You're a person of science, Dr. Sato," Wei said. "*You* tell me what to believe."

"Is this...is this you?"

The young man looked around. "You see another bene-factor willing to give you a second chance? Appearances are misleading. My age is irrelevant. What really matters is the next sixty seconds."

"Sixty seconds?"

"Yes. Will you spend them arguing and complaining, or will you convince me you were worth ten minutes of my precious time?"

Selene's expression blanched. "You...you really are an investor? How did you find out about my research?"

"It's beside the point." Wei glanced at his wristwatch. "Forty seconds."

Selene looked toward the garbage bin. "Okay," she said. "Okay, I'll do it."

She breathed in, hoping that the chip hadn't been broken. She raised her right hand and waited. One...two... five seconds. The piece of the bottle that still had the label attached hovered toward her. It fell gently into her palm, like a leaf carried by the wind.

"Fascinating," Wei said. He was typing something on a small device he picked from his pocket. "The resonance waves are practically invisible, and the connection is stable. Just the thing I need."

The rain was falling more heavily now. Selene wiped her face with the back of her hand.

"Who do you work for?"

"For humanity's sake," Wei said. "How would you like to

join a group of extraordinary people I'm assembling to change the face of the world?"

"Extraordinary people?"

"People like you, Doctor: someone willing to do whatever it takes to prove that the impossible is only a possibility that has not yet been discovered. Interloop is your brainchild. I'm offering you the chance to unlock its potential."

"Why?"

"Why not? I have the means and the resources, and I'm interested in the technology. Do you need to know more?"

"What's the catch?"

"There isn't one, but you'll have to give me an answer soon. Once this boat sails, it doesn't go back."

Wei handed her a business card. It was blank on both sides, except for a strip of text showing a geographical coordinate and a date.

"Be there if you're interested in giving Interloop a future. Otherwise, I suggest you learn how to make real coffee. I tried your espresso, and I wasn't impressed." Wei turned and started walking away.

"You still haven't told me who you really are."

"I did tell you."

"That wasn't an answer."

"How about this?" Wei opened an umbrella. "I'm your second chance at making history, Dr. Sato. For now, that'll have to be enough."

He turned the corner and disappeared from view.

3

BIRGER

(ONE WEEK LATER)

The flight lasted almost seven hours. She spent them looking out the helicopter window, wondering what the hell she was thinking when she signed off on the kid's proposal.

"Bring heavy clothes." That was the only message Wei sent her, two hours before her scheduled departure.

Bring heavy clothes.

Brilliant. She was going somewhere cold. Very helpful. That excluded about half the planet.

She barely knew this guy's name, and already hated his guts.

"We're here!"

The pilot's voice startled her. She adjusted her headphones and lifted a thumb.

The pilot—a middle-aged man with a bushy beard and a frown embedded on his forehead—hadn't exactly been the ideal traveling companion. Every question she'd asked had been answered the same way: "Sorry, Doc. I'm just paid to fly."

Good talk.

When they landed, Selene stepped out of the helicopter and a gust of freezing air cut off her breath. She nearly dropped her hand luggage in surprise.

Snow-capped mountains and rocky hills were all around her. Long stretches of frozen water shimmered against the sunlight. The air was dry, sharp as a knife's blade.

A tall man with dark skin and a big, squashed nose was waiting for her next to a snow crawler big enough to carry a dozen people.

"Dr. Sato?" he asked in a thick accent.

"Yeah, it's me."

"I'm Johan." He picked up her bag and tossed it in the crawler's trunk.

"Follow me. I'll take you to the center."

"The center? What center?"

"I'm sorry. I'm just paid to drive."

Selene breathed out through her teeth. *Awesome. Another chatterbox.*

The crawler ate mile after mile of the iced, desolate vastness. For the first thirty minutes, Selene tried to strike a conversation with the driver, but it was like trying to peel a marble statue with her fingernails.

She gave up, and instead tried to find a comfortable position in her seat that kept shifting slightly as they moved forward. She hadn't been able to sleep in the helicopter, and couldn't remember the last time she'd actually rested.

The past few days had been a quick succession of events that seemed to belong to someone else's life.

After accepting Wei's job, she sold her car and everything else she owned. She hadn't stopped to consider the implications of her decision, and said yes knowing nothing about what was waiting for her.

She was so desperate to turn her life on its head that she

made the same mistake twice. Giving the finger to Ben had been a rushed decision, one she'd made without thinking. Accepting Wei's proposal had been no different. A part of her expected to regret it soon.

The constant motion of the vehicle lulled her, made it difficult to concentrate. She looked outside the window, to a world made of an endless succession of white peaks and gray hills that offered nothing interesting to see.

She closed her eyes for what seemed like a few seconds and jolted awake when the vehicle stopped.

"We're here," the driver announced.

Selene blinked. She looked up at the sky, which had turned a dark shade of blue. The sun was a squashed ball pressed to the horizon. How long had she slept? Two, three hours? More?

Outside, the landscape had changed little. A chain of snow-crowned mountains stared back at her. Ice and rocks and snow were pretty much all there was.

To her left, a collection of medium-sized hills stood out against the topaz-blue sky. A strange stalagmite-shaped rock formation stood a few dozen yards away from their vehicle. Selene narrowed her eyes. Her heart skipped a beat when she realized it wasn't a rock formation at all; it was a spiral-shaped building.

It had to be at least five hundred feet tall. The silver-gray metal was shiny and reflected the light like iron pyrite.

"What is this place?" Selene asked.

When she turned toward the driver, he had already started the vehicle.

"Hello? I'm talking to you!"

The crawler sped up, lifting a large amount of ice as it moved away.

"Hey!" Selene stared at the vehicle, a freezing wind

slicing through her coat like a ghost blade. "Why is nobody talking to me?"

"Hello, Dr. Sato."

Selene turned sharply. A man with a neatly trimmed goatee was smiling at her.

"To answer your question," he continued, "this is the Valhalla Center. Welcome to your new home."

Without her noticing, he'd picked up the luggage the driver had unloaded from the crawler.

"Great." Selene studied the stranger. "So at least one of you can talk."

"Sorry for the lack of information, Doctor. It's the way we do things around here."

Selene assessed the stranger. He was wearing an azure uniform that was unlike anything Selene had seen before. On his leather belt was attached a set of keys, a walkie-talkie, and a large pistol.

"My name is Birger." He held out his hand and Selene shook it. "I will be your liaison for as long as you are with us."

"Liaison?"

"In case you need to contact Wei."

"You mean like a buffer? Why? Can't he sort through his calls like anyone else?"

"Wei is a very busy person. He needs a reliable way to filter out priority messages."

"Okay. So you're my filter."

"Among other things. If you need anything for your research, I'm the guy to call."

"And what's that for?" Selene pointed to the gun.

"This is just a precaution." Birger started moving toward the building. "How was your trip?"

"Long," Selene said, feeling more like herself after the

nap. "Is there a reason for keeping your employees in the dark? I mean, am I going to work for the Pentagon or something?"

If Birger noticed the annoyance in her tone, he didn't show it. "We've a safety protocol to implement every time we add a new member to the team. Wei doesn't enjoy taking risks."

"Risks?" Selene glanced at the frozen landscape. "You expect Santa Claus to steal one of your secrets?"

"Valhalla is the hub of some of the world's most cutting-edge technologies, Doctor. Isolation and secrecy protect its discoveries from many risks."

Selene frowned as she looked at the building in the middle of nowhere. "You mean there's more than one of these?"

"There are three centers similar to Valhalla on three different continents. Two more are being built as we speak."

Selene whistled. "And why did I end up at this one?"

"Your skills will be put to good use here. Are you tired? Do you wish to rest?"

"I'm good."

"In that case, I'll show you the lab first, then your quarters."

A pathway carved into the ice led them to the building's main entrance. Two armed men guarded it.

Now that she was closer to the building, Selene noticed a tenuous, almost invisible green halo shrouding the entrance.

Birger took a metal badge from his pocket and handed it to Selene. "Pin this to your chest."

"What is it?"

"A portable deflector. You'll need it to pass through the entrance."

Selene was about to ask why when she realized what the green halo was. She pinned the badge on her chest and followed her guide.

The halo phased out as they passed and came back on immediately after they stepped inside the building. Birger exchanged a few words with the guards, who nodded and then let them in.

"A force field?" Selene nodded toward the entrance.

"Yes," Birger said. "It's a Lambda Trust."

"A Lambda Trust? I thought they were still being tested."

"Not in Valhalla. Since we created them, we have a good grip on the technology."

"*You* created them?" Selene stopped mid-stride. "Wait a second. The Utaru Industries came up with them. They are based in Montreal, aren't they? They publicized the damn thing so much I can hardly remember anything else in the past two months."

Birger smiled. "Wei sold the license to the highest bidder. The Utaru won the auction. With the proceeds, he could pay for the construction of the centers I mentioned earlier. Are you coming?"

"Okay, slow down. You talk about that kid as if he did it all by himself."

"Of course he didn't," Birger replied. "Well, I suppose in a way he did. The Lambda Trust was his idea and he put his money in the project, paid the people to come up with a viable way of making it happen, and tested it in this very center. Now why don't we keep moving? There is a lot you need to see."

Birger resumed walking without waiting for a reply.

Selene followed him.

The interior of the building was a succession of marble columns interspersed with large arches. They passed a large hallway with a reception desk. Every so often, they would encounter a person wearing a white coat or a blue jumpsuit. The liaison waved at them or gave a quick nod.

"You expect me to believe that little smartass handles all this?" Selene lowered her voice so that only the liaison could hear her. "I mean...come on! Who's helping him?"

"It's a comment I hear a lot." A burly guard approached Birger and handed him a piece of paper. The liaison read it quickly, then dismissed the man and kept walking. "Wei doesn't answer to anyone, but knows how to surround himself with the right people. He couldn't advance his projects without help. That's why you're here. That's why he needs you."

They reached an elevator encased on the side of a long corridor. Birger placed his badge on the control panel and the doors swung open. Inside the cabin, he pushed the button B3. The elevator started moving up.

"When can I talk to him?" Selene asked.

"About what?"

"About *this*." Selene spread her arms. "All he told me about this place was to bring some damn heavy clothes with me."

Birger blinked. "Hmm. Why am I not surprised?"

"You're smiling. What is it? Some rite of passage newbies have to go through to be part of the pack?"

"Wei often forgets that normal people need more information than he thinks."

"Really? You mean, that message... He didn't mean to be funny?"

"I wouldn't bet my secret stash of brownies on it, but I'm inclined to say no. He didn't do it on purpose. Regardless, you don't have to worry about anything. There's a reason I'm here. Like I said, my job is to facilitate your staying in Valhalla, providing anything you need."

Selene eyed Birger's gun. "And maybe shoot someone now and then?"

"You have an interesting way of asking questions."

"You have an interesting way of avoiding them."

"Touché." Birger smiled. "Wei is a careful person. He'd be willing to do anything in order to safeguard his projects. I'm in charge of the security team."

"It almost sounds as if you're expecting trouble. Isn't that a bit paranoid, considering where we are? In the middle of nowhere?"

"Better to be paranoid than run out of ammo when you need it."

Selene smiled at that. "Touché," she said.

"I don't know when you can talk to Wei," Birger said. "He left the day before yesterday for Pretoria. A business trip that will keep him busy until September. We won't see him for a while."

The elevator door opened, and they stepped outside.

"Okay. This is plan B3," Birger said. "*Your* plan."

"*My* plan?"

"Yes, doctor. The B3 is entirely reserved for the developing of Interloop."

Selene stared at the liaison. In the Evan Den Bawer Institute, she was allowed to use a couple repurposed classrooms smaller than her bedroom. This was the entire floor of a huge building. She counted at least a half-dozen rooms just from where she was standing.

"I don't... I mean. Are you sure? *All of it*?"

"All of it. If you need more assets, let me know."

"Oh, I will."

"Good. This way. I'll show you around. Wei instructed your team to follow whatever protocols and system you have in place for the testing of—"

"Whoa, Whoa. Wait a second. No one said anything about a *team*."

"Well, another lack of communication. Sorry about that. Wei hired the best engineers and technicians money could buy to assist you with the developing of Interloop."

"You don't say."

"Of course, if you think the staff isn't qualified, I can arrange a round of interviews to select someone more suitable. Wei figured it'd save you time having a team ready from the get-go."

"Well, the kid is not wrong. I hate wasting time."

"Good to know. This way."

Selene struggled to focus on the tour. Being there, on *her* floor, felt like waking up from a year-long nightmare to live inside a dream that belonged to someone else.

"Doctor?"

Selene blinked. "Sorry," she said. "I spaced. What did you say?"

"I was asking if you needed anything else?"

"You could pinch me really hard, I guess."

"I'm sorry?"

"Never mind. I'm just trying to wrap my head around all this. How is it possible that that kid has access to these kind of resources?" She pointed to the expensive equipment all around them.

Birger held her stare with an expression of calculated calm. This told Selene that it wasn't the first time someone asked him that question.

"It's difficult to explain," he said.

"Try me."

"I've been working for Wei for almost two years," he said. "He has a gift. He makes things happen. When you're around him, it feels like anything is possible. If you'll be with us for long enough, you'll get what I mean. I promise you."

4

PUZZLE

(2025)

Two months had passed since the helicopter left her on that frozen wasteland. The strangest, most nerve-wracking and exhausting two months of her life.

The time spent in the Valhalla Research Center felt surreal, like a vision that blurred into a dream.

In the morning, when she woke up in her apartment, it still took her a few seconds to realize where she was.

Every time her eyes opened, she expected to stare at the gray wall of a basement, the sickening smell of old carpet signaling the beginning of a new day.

Instead, she now woke up to wonder and possibilities. She had unlimited resources for her projects, and no one to answer to. No budget cuts. No bureaucratic crap to slow her down. Just pure, unchallenged research freedom.

Hard to believe a twenty-year-old made it possible.

She had spoken with Wei only on three occasions, and for only ten minutes. She'd gathered from those brief meetings that the kid hated wasting time.

Something they both had in common.

It's hard to get a feel for a person you just meet for a few minutes, but Selene was starting to understand what Birger meant about Wei.

He was much more than his appearance suggested. The staff at the center called him the Genius Boy. Stories about him abounded, but half of what she'd gathered seemed like a lot of hooey.

What mattered to Selene was that Wei's resources allowed her team to make progress quickly. They had effectively tested the Interloop technology on several objects with a wide range of weight and mass. The Interlink signal's strength and the frequency loophole—two of the biggest issues she had never solved—had been put to rest.

She was now ready to move on to the next phase: the creation of a viable prototype.

But despite these successes, a thought stole her sleep.

Since living in Valhalla, she'd only been able to access floor B3 and the main floor, where the cafeteria and other common areas were located.

What happened on other floors remained a mystery. The elevator wouldn't even allow her to get anywhere other than floor B3.

"Security reasons, Doctor." That had been Birger's reply when she asked him why other parts of the building were off-limits.

"Can you elaborate?"

"Each floor is a separate section contributing to a different project. There is no need for you to know what's happening outside of B3."

"You mean each floor except B10?"

Birger had raised his eyebrow at that statement. Evidently, he hadn't expected Selene to know about B10. She had learned of it by overhearing a conversation at the gym.

Well, "overhearing" wasn't the right word. She had stalked a couple guys when she had realized what they were talking about.

"You are right." Birger hadn't denied the existence of the floor. He probably knew that some things couldn't be hidden forever from a person who spent months in the center. "On Bio are the collected, analyzed, and implemented breakthroughs made by the individual floors."

"Implemented for *what*? Wait, let me guess. That's classified information, right?"

"I'm afraid so."

"This is bullshit. I know that all the employees have signed a non-disclosure agreement."

"That's correct."

"Then what are you guys so afraid of?"

"Curiosity might prevail over the risk of repercussions. Valhalla is the forge of many groundbreaking discoveries, Doctor. Some of the best minds in the world are working within these walls. Do you understand? Keeping discoveries a secret is not only a precaution, it's an assurance that Valhalla's secrets will remain so."

Despite the liaison staying tight-lipped, Selene had tried several times to get him to talk. It'd been like trying to convince a waterfall to flow backward.

Now, after months in the dark, curiosity was eating her up. She felt like Pandora, the legendary woman who was gifted a closed box with instructions not to open it.

But Selene hadn't given up. She had asked questions to fellow team members and colleagues to find out if anyone knew more about Bio, or why Valhalla existed. Unfortunately, no one seemed interested in answering that question. The indifference of her colleagues drove her crazy. Why were they happy to work blindfolded? Didn't they want to know?

When Selene had signed the working agreement, she'd given up all rights to use Interloop technology for a large monetary reward. Which meant that once the technology had been tested and implemented, Selene would have no way of knowing how Wei would use her invention.

That hadn't bothered her until now. *Now* she was suspecting something. Judging by the tests Wei asked her to perform, one thing was certain: the kid didn't want to use Interloop in the entertainment industries, or in media-related projects, as she had believed at the beginning.

A couple of navy officers contacted her in the year she spent looking for investors. The demands they had made concerning Interloop's viability and implementation were very similar to Wei's.

She suspected that the Genius Boy wanted to use Interloop for military purposes.

5

SEIEN

(ONE MONTH LATER)

Selene was supposed to be celebrating.

That morning, her team had successfully tested the first prototype of Quantum Interloop, a device stable enough to be integrated with whatever Wei was working on at floor Bio.

And yet Selene was unhappy.

The end of the project meant that her assignment in Valhalla was over. Birger had informed her that her departure was scheduled for the next week.

Every time she thought about the end of her contract, she felt like punching someone in the face.

She had every reason to feel accomplished. Interloop was a reality. She had proven that her invention could be used, and that someone was willing to pay good money for it.

It was a victory. Then why did she feel like shit?

The doorbell rang twice. "Come in," she said.

Birger stepped into her apartment with a bouquet. "Dr. Sato," the liaison greeted her. "Hope I'm not disturbing."

Selene teased a smile. "Birger, I didn't take you for the romantic type."

Birger blushed. "What? No. You've misunderstood. I don't..." He trailed off, then studied her expression. "You're making fun of me, aren't you?"

"Glad that three months together taught you some humor." Selene took the flowers and smelled the fragrance; exotic and pungent.

"They're from Wei," Birger said. "He's thrilled with the excellent work you've done."

As Selene was putting the flower in a jar, she blinked. A couple of them had odd star-shaped petals. "What flowers are these? I've never seen them before."

"That's because they are custom made."

Selene frowned. "Say what?"

"Wei commissioned them from a geneticist specifically for you."

Selene stared at Birger for a good half-minute. "You mean they're *Una Tantum*?"

"Exactly."

"They must have cost a fortune!"

"They are a token of appreciation for your hard work," Birger said. "The *other* token was transferred into your bank account a couple seconds ago."

Selene tapped at her cellphone's display. "What?" She stared at Birger with a confused expression. "This can't be right. It's more than double what I was promised."

"Wei felt compelled to be generous. After all, you completed the project in half the time agreed upon."

Selene had to sit in a chair. "I...I don't even know what to do with all this money."

"My advice would be to start with a vacation. Perhaps

somewhere warmer. Somewhere with a beach, and a long line of palm trees as far as the eye can see."

Selene looked at her cell, her head spinning.

"Well, I should be going." The liaison smiled. "It was a pleasure working with you, Doctor. Have a good life." He turned and made to leave.

"Birger?"

The man stopped and looked over his shoulder. "Yes, Doctor?"

"I want to be a part of it."

"I'm sorry?"

"Valhalla. Whatever's being developed here, I want to be a part of it."

Birger's smile was equal parts confusion and amusement. "I don't understand."

"I want to work in Bio."

The liaison blinked. "This wasn't the arrangement. You know perfectly well that your contract—"

"I know what's written on that piece of paper." Selene felt her heart pounding. She needed to make him see how much she wanted this. "Wei can take back every dollar he gave me. I'm willing to work for free. I don't care about money. Something extraordinary is happening in this place, and I want to be a part of it."

Birger cleared his throat. "Your...enthusiasm is flattering, Doctor. Unfortunately, I'm afraid we just can't accommodate—"

"Look at me, Birger. I'm begging you."

"Doctor—"

"Listen. All my life I wanted to be part of something bigger than me, something that mattered. Something like Valhalla. Now I've finally found it. Please. If I could just talk to Wei—"

"Wei is busy."

"But—"

"And I know his answer would be no."

"He'll be back in Valhalla in a couple days. I just need five minutes of his time. It's all I'm asking."

Birger shook his head. "He left instructions not to be disturbed. I'm sorry. I'll send him your regards."

Selene made to reply, but the liaison turned and walked out of the room before she could speak.

She sank into the chair, her breathing unsteady. She reached for her cell. The screen was showing a six-digit number. It was more than she had earned in the past five years combined.

She closed her eyes and imagined opening the doors to Ben's office and showing him the amount. She could see the principal's eyes widening as he realized the opportunity he had lost.

When she opened her eyes again, the triumphant image had vanished in the smoke of a memory that would never be.

That Selene, the broken woman who wanted to prove she was right, would have taken Wei's money and never looked back.

But Valhalla had changed her. She now knew that there was more to life than a substantial paycheck. There was the sheer pleasure of discovery through infinite possibilities.

She couldn't remember the last time she'd woken up an hour earlier, glad to go to work. Who was she kidding? It hadn't been *work* to her! It had been an adventure.

To the new Selene, Wei's money felt like Judas' thirty pieces of silver. It felt like giving up her soul after finding Paradise.

She stared at the cell's screen, eyes glassy. Maybe she was

making the mistake of her life, but she was going to do it with eyes wide open.

She moved her fingers across the screen. The amount disappeared from her bank account and returned to the sender.

SELENE GOT on the BIO floor by sheer luck.

She was returning to the lab to complete one of her last reports when she bumped into a technician running to the cafeteria.

"I'm sorry," the man said, helping her to her feet.

"It's okay." Selene rubbed her shoulder. "I'll live."

The technician apologized again, then headed for the cafeteria without realizing his badge had fallen on the floor.

Selene picked it up and read the ID. The man worked at BIO.

She started to call him, then snapped her mouth shut. She glanced at the badge, held hostage by a thought.

There it was. The universe gave her the chance to answer all her questions. She would not lose it.

All she had to do now was risk her career on account of her curiosity.

Lunchtime was the only time of the day the floors were empty of most of their staff.

It's now or never.

When the doors of the elevator closed, Selene inhaled sharply. "Please make this work." She pressed the badge to the panel and, after the longest second of her life, the elevator started moving.

"Yes!"

The door opened to a wide corridor. She looked around,

paying attention to any noise that might suggest someone was there.

This floor was almost identical to B3. Same floor plan, same control panels, even the length of the corridors was the same. Now all she had to do was to find...

"...without paying attention to the density of the noberium, for example. We had to..."

Selene stepped back and pressed herself against the wall. Two engineers turned the corner, missing her by mere steps.

When their voices became inaudible, she risked a glance. The corridor was clear.

"Jesus. That was close." She resumed walking.

Each floor's centralized information unit was stored in a room called the *Node*. Selene hoped that was the case also for Bio.

She kept walking and found the door she was looking for. Carefully, she pressed her ear to it. No voices, no suspicious noises. She stepped inside and closed the door behind her.

There was little time. The technicians would be back from lunch soon.

The room was dimly lit by the control panels, LEDs, and a couple table lamps. Selene sat down behind the nearest control unit and began typing on the keyboard.

Her eyes darted as she read the content of the files.

...carbondurene alloy-reinforced noberium seems to be an ideal candidate for the armor...

...the force field tests have produced encouraging results. Unfortunately, we haven't resolved the phase-shifting issue for the...

...gravimetric bubble is still far from being created to specifications...

...and the energy saber proved versatile enough to be considered as a close combat weapon in the final design of the...

"Give Selene Sato a finger, and she'll take the whole arm."

Selene turned sharply toward the familiar voice. "Wei?"

The young man looked at her with just the hint of a smile. "The one and only."

"How did you get in here?" Selene glanced at the door, which had stayed closed the entire time.

"You're assuming I wasn't already in."

"What? You...you mean you knew I was coming? How?"

Wei shrugged. "Keep the door to the chicken coop open, and the fox will get in."

"I see." Selene inhaled slowly. "That technician didn't lose his badge by chance, did he?"

"There is no such thing as chance, only a series of events that bring us closer to the person we're meant to be."

"Poetic, really. I'm about to tear up. Why did you do it?"

"Why? Were you expecting a job interview?"

"I was expecting an answer, not a goddamned game. What am I to you? A lab rat?"

"I think you're desperate, and desperate people show their true colors."

"You think I'm desperate?"

"You tell me. Aren't you someone who's willing to risk everything to be part of my project?"

"You've figured that out *now*? You knew it already! I told you a thousand times. You just had to take my word for it."

"The road to hell is paved with words, promises, and good intentions. No thanks. I trust only extreme actions and unavoidable consequences."

"All right. I'm here. I've been tested. What happens now? Am I on board?"

"Not so fast." Wei typed in a code on the console Selene had used. "Coming here proved to me you have guts. Curiosity despite the risks is something I value, but there will be a price to pay if you continue to work in Valhalla."

"What price?"

"Your freedom, for starters. You won't be able to live a civilian life for years. Are you willing to do that?"

"I have nothing left behind. I'm ready."

"Ready?" Wei smiled. "You've no idea what that word means. Not yet."

Wei pulled something out of his pocket. In the semi-darkness of the room, it took Selene a few seconds to realize it was a gun.

"Whoa, what's that for?"

Wei handed her the weapon. "Take it."

"What?"

"I said take it."

"Are you high?"

"You want to go all the way? Then take the gun."

Selene looked at him. He wasn't joking. "What the hell do you want to prove by—"

"You're the one who needs to prove something, and it all starts by taking this gun. Come on. I haven't got all day."

Selene bit her lip.

"Last chance."

She reached for the weapon and took it.

"Good." With a sudden move, Wei forced the barrel of the gun onto his forehead. "Now pull the trigger."

"Are you *insane*? Let go of me!"

"Did I stutter? Pull the trigger."

"Are you out of your goddamn mind?"

"I'm trying to understand something. Come on. Do it."

Selene tried to free herself from Wei's grip, but he was stronger than she had expected.

"Why do you want me to shoot you?"

"Because I like you, and I want to give you a chance to prove you aren't a loser."

"A loser?"

"Who are you now? The failed researcher who got booted, or the barista who couldn't make a decent espresso if her life depended on it?"

"Are you trying to piss me off? Look, I'm not going to—"

"Or the loser who drank half a bottle of wine to get a good night's sleep?"

"I just want to—"

"There weren't mirrors in your basement, were there?"

Selene blinked. "What?"

"I thought so. It's strange. I've never seen a house with no mirrors."

"How the hell do you know what—"

"I have a theory. You didn't have the guts to look at yourself. You didn't want to look at a loser."

Selene clenched her teeth. "You don't know shit about me."

"You wasted one year of your life begging for someone who could keep Interloop on life support. I know you failed. I had to pick you and your dead project from the garbage bin. You were so pathetic it made me sick to my stomach."

"Don't—"

"Don't you understand? You sold me Interloop for pennies on the dollar. Tell me, Doctor Sato. How does it feel to beg to be part of something bigger than yourself?"

"Shut up."

"Does it hurt?"

"I said, shut up!"

"In here, you look around and see something you'd die to create, something you wish was *yours*. Valhalla is the dream you didn't get to live because you didn't have the guts to get enough nays. What a waste. I don't know whether to laugh or cry."

Wei had removed his hands from the gun. Now Selene was holding the weapon by herself.

"You're a loser, Doctor. A desperate loser."

"I'm not."

"No? Then pull the trigger and prove me wrong. Prove to me you're willing to do whatever it takes to be part of Valhalla."

Selene wanted to do it. She wanted to pull the trigger. That realization shook her to the core. She wanted to kill somebody because he said the truth, a truth she avoided for too long.

He's right.

Selene was breathing fast, cold sweat pouring down her forehead.

He's right. You holed up in universities and institutes for years, thinking you were making a difference, when you were simply working for someone who wanted a check with as many zeros as possible. You sold out your ideas, and you never had the decency to admit it.

"I don't need to prove anything." She dropped the gun on the table. "You're right. I'm a loser. I've always hoped to come across something like Valhalla, to work for someone like *you*. And now that I've found all this, I can't think of my life without being part of it." She looked down at the gun. "It'd be easier to put a bullet in my head."

Wei looked at her. "You're wrong," he said.

"What do you mean? You just said that—"

"You're not a loser, but you needed those words to come

out of your mouth to believe them. You needed to exorcise your demons. Doesn't it feel better now?"

"You did *this* to boost my self-esteem?"

"Did I succeed?"

Selene shook her head, then smiled. "Yeah. I guess so."

"Good. Now I can welcome you to the inner circle of Valhalla." Wei picked up the gun.

"So it was a test?"

"I prefer the word *catharsis*."

"Catharsis?" Selene raised an eyebrow. "If you say so. But I want to make something absolutely clear."

"What is that?"

Selene looked at the weapon. "I didn't believe for a second that it was loaded."

"Really?" Wei aimed the gun up and pulled the trigger. The bullet went through the ceiling and pieces of plaster fell all around them.

Selene stepped back, her eyes fixed on the hole. "Jesus Christ! I could have killed you!"

"History isn't made with *could haves*." Wei picked up his cellphone. "Birger? Send a maintenance guy to Node Bio. There's some cleaning to be done."

"Roger that."

Selene couldn't banish the smile creeping across her face. "You're crazy."

"I prefer the term *visionary*, but I could live with *messiah* or *savior*."

"How about *blowhard*?"

"I've been called worse."

"Well, okay. What happens now?"

"Now, Doctor, you've earned yourself a peek down the rabbit hole. Follow me."

SELENE RAISED A TREMBLING HAND, touching the armor that covered the mannequin.

Smooth. Solid. Pulsing with energy. She had seen nothing like it.

"What's this?"

Wei had his arms crossed. "A prototype of a multifunctional battle-exosuit made of carbondurene alloy and reinforced noberium coating."

Selene whistled. "Impressive... I think. That mouthful explains absolutely nothing to me."

"My technicians have little imagination for naming things—especially cool things. I call it *Seien*."

"Seien?"

"A neologism I coined from Japanese. It means: 'Wall of Stars.'"

"Pretty," Selene said, looking at the armor. "So, what's it for?"

Wei started pacing around the room, hands clasped behind his back. He looked much older than before. "We live in a complicated world, and my actions will contribute to complicating it in the coming years. Knowing that this exosuit exists helps me sleep at night. If things go south, this Seien will prove one of the best investments I ever made."

"Things? What things?"

"I have plans, Doctor. Projects that will contribute to bettering humankind. Regretfully, some of these projects are seen as a threat by some."

"Who are you talking about?"

"You could call them competitors."

"When you say *threat*, what do you mean? Threat in what way?"

"I wish I had a straight answer. Threat in many ways, I suppose. I secretly hope that I will never have to use this exosuit. But I can't risk not having it."

"I'm confused. Why are you showing me a battle suit you hope you'll never use?"

"Because I want to put you in charge of Bio. I want you to run the Valhalla Project."

Selene stared at the Genius Boy for a long time. "What?" she blurted.

"You showed a rare talent for coping with problems. Interloop was just a test. Now the real challenge begins." Wei pointed to the armor. "My technicians have been working on this prototype for years. Unfortunately, they are making very slow progress."

"And you think I could do better?"

"You wouldn't be here otherwise."

"What do you want me to do exactly?"

"Make it functional as soon as possible." Wei rested his hands on the exosuit. "Believe me, it won't be easy. The Seien is made up of hundreds of different parts, and your Interloop is just the last item on a very long list. Each of the components must work in synergy to function properly. The Seien needs to work as a cohesive unit of different parts. It needs to respond to the pilot's commands as if it were a second skin."

"Hundreds of different parts, you said. So *this* is what the other floors are working on?"

"Yes. Each floor works on a specific component. Durability, technology, usability, energy, you name it. Then Bio processes all the information and moves the project forward."

"So it's like putting together a puzzle."

"You could say that. It won't be a walk in the park to

make it functional. Some technologies needed to power the exosuit still need to be invented. We're talking about years of experimentation. If you're not sure you want to be a part of this, tell me now. This is a long-term program. Many have called it a far-fetched fantasy. It has broken more than one will. Three project coordinators quit on me, the last one less than a week ago."

"So that's why I'm here. You need a replacement."

"I don't just need a replacement. I need someone who will do the job. It's going to be hard, Doctor. Some of the brightest people I know tried and failed. Don't take this offer lightly. I can show more information if you need to—"

"I don't need to know anything else." Selene assumed a wide, open stance. "I'm ready."

Wei cocked an eyebrow. "Are you sure? I didn't really tell you anything about—"

"I don't need to know," she repeated. "All I care about is an obstacle to overcome, and that you need me to take care of it. When do we start?"

PART II

HELLHOUND

6

CHOICES

(2028)

uck. Time's a bitch.

Three years, seven months, and four days. It seemed only yesterday that the Genius Boy had offered her the job.

She had been working *for* him back then. Now Selene was working *with* him.

The simple shift of prepositions had revolutionized Selene's world.

After all that time, she still wasn't sure if accepting Wei's offer had been the best or the worst decision of her life. Maybe it had been both.

"Doctor?" The engineer sitting behind the console station was staring at her. His eyebrows were locked in a frown.

He wasn't the only one looking at her with expectation. There were ten more people in the control room, dressed in the same white coat, black shirt, and blue tie he was wearing. All were looking at her like a bunch of altar boys waiting for the priest to recite his sermon.

Selene cleared her throat. "Can you repeat that, control?"

"The zodiac is ready," the engineer said, pointing to the woman standing on the other side of the shatterproof glass.

"What are her vitals?" Selene asked.

"Nominal." The engineer glanced at the flat screen. "Biometrics are in the green. She's good to go."

Selene looked at the person standing in the other room and shivered. She could only imagine what she was feeling.

Selene breathed in, crossing her arms tightly against her chest. *Zodiac. A poetic way of calling her a goddamned lab rat.*

Everyone was waiting for her. It was time.

"Deborah," she spoke to the woman via interlink. "Are you ready?"

"I was born ready, Doc. Hit me."

Selene hesitated. Once she gave the order, there was no turning back.

The shitty feeling of helplessness hit her like a brick. Every time it made her sick to her stomach. It was like ordering a friend to take a walk through a minefield.

They needed more time. There were still too many things that could go wrong.

Unfortunately, Wei didn't feel the same way. He was pushing to get the exosuit ready as soon as possible. That meant leaving her to deal with the collaterals.

Selene stared at the woman she'd been working with for the past five months. She was brave, as smart as a whip, and thought well under pressure. She was also the best zodiac they ever had.

It was a difficult and dangerous job, no way around it. The Seien were the most complex and powerful ion-powered cybernetic exosuits ever built. They could increase a person's speed and strength by a factor of ten, enhance stamina and alertness, and keep a human being alive and alert with damages that would bring anyone to the hospital.

And that was just scratching the surface.

The exosuit could create a force field as a defense mechanism, could shoot a plasma blast able to penetrate five feet of titanium, and could create an energy saber that would have been the envy of a Jedi knight. The bad news was that most of these parts were still unstable.

At this stage, wearing a Seien was like wearing a suicide vest. One mistake could be fatal.

Jesus Christ. Please make this work.

Selene took a deep breath. "Deborah," she said, steadying her voice. "Begin the donning."

"Roger that, Doc."

The zodiac moved into position, stepping inside the red circle painted ten feet away from the armor-clad mannequin placed at the far end of the room.

"All right." Selene bit the inside of her mouth. "Give me the status, people. Systems?"

"Go, operator," a technician answered while reading the string of data on his console station. "Ego-Seien connection established."

"Field?"

"Go, operator," another man said. "Exofuel activated and rolling. Proximity buffer triggered."

Selene wet her lips. She tasted blood where she bit too hard. This was the first risk. Once the connection was established, Deborah needed to direct the pieces remotely onto herself via the Interloop.

"Reading?"

"Seien activated, operator. The zodiac is commencing the summoning."

Inside the other room, Deborah spread her arms and legs as if preparing to stop a boulder. Then it happened.

Pieces of armor detached from the mannequin like a storm of hornets from a nest and flew toward the zodiac.

Selene gripped the edges of the console station, trying to breathe normally. It wasn't easy. The Seien's largest parts—the breastplate and the visor—weighed several pounds. If they deviated from the intended trajectory, they could dislocate a shoulder or break a bone.

It had happened before.

The armor swirled around the zodiac. One by one, each component—visor, shoulder strap, breastplate, back, thigh plate, and skirt—slid into the micro-fittings of the powered undersuit that acted as a buffer between the heavy armor and the girl's body.

"Status?"

"Hooks on, operator. Quantum Interloop stable."

"All right." Selene released her grip from the console, ignoring her sweaty palms. "Hit her."

"Roger that, operator. Launcher in the room."

A tennis ball launcher that had been sitting on the other side of the room was powered on.

"Engaging."

A tennis ball flew across the room and was about to hit Deborah when a flash of light surrounded the zodiac and the object deviated from its trajectory, slamming into the glass wall.

"Reading?"

"A fifth of K.T. field," a team member answered.

"Okay. That was warming up, Deborah," Selene said via interlink. "Let's try again. This time, give me an all-the-way barrier."

"With pleasure, Doc."

The second time, the force field lasted longer and was more visible, like a distant blue halo surrounding the exosuit. As a result, the next tennis ball was not merely deflected, but repelled and thrown against the tennis launcher itself.

"That's what I'm talking about." Selene turned toward the technician sitting next to her. "All right. Let's bump this up and try the five-pound med ball."

"Roger that, operator. Five-pound medicine ball in the launcher."

The test went on for the next thirty minutes. Each time heavier objects were thrown against the exosuit-generated barrier, the last of which was a fifteen-pound weight.

The zodiac repelled with increasing precision all objects.

Selene kept her expectations low. They were simply stretching the ion engine for the real test.

"Deborah." Selene checked the data appearing on her console. "How are you feeling?"

"I'm the kingpin, Doc. Throw me the Moon, and I'll punch it all the way to Saturn."

"Let's keep the Moon for now," Selene said, smiling. "The Earth's axis wouldn't be the same without it, and I like my seasons the way they are. You're doing great out there, and your bios are stellar. You feel like crossing the threshold?"

A short stretch of silence, then Deborah's voice came through strong and clear. "Yeah. Punch me, Doc."

Selene turned to the technician on the far side of the control room.

"Weaponry," she said. "Let's get this rolling."

"Roger that, operator. Activating fire mouth."

A bigger, heavier object that looked like a small cannon replaced the ball launcher.

"Fire mouth on standby," the weaponry station said. "Blast energy level calibrated to one-tenth of impulse."

"Suit up, guys!" Selene picked a head visor and signaled the others to do the same. "It's go time."

There was a shuffling sound as everyone grabbed protection from the safety locker and then went back to their control stations.

"Deborah?" Selene said. "The moment you feel something's off with the hardware, I want to know."

"Copy that, Doc. I won't push it."

Selene looked to her left. "Control?"

"All systems are green. Bios looks good."

"All right." Selene raised a hand. She breathed in and then exhaled. "Fire!"

The cannon shot an emerald beam against the exosuit's shield.

"Control? Give me an ongoing reading."

"Structural integrity at seventy percent, operator. No focal loss in sight."

"Increase beam power by agreed baseline every fifteen seconds."

"Roger that, operator. Focal beam increasing. Five... seven...nine percent..."

The beam's power increased visibly. Selene read Deborah's biometrics: increased heartbeat, dilation of the pupils... Everything looked tight but still viable. No red flags yet.

"Deborah? How are things going?"

The girl's voice was interspersed by static. "It's like... Fourth of July here, Doc...can do this all day."

"Her parameters are within the safety range, operator," a staff member said, answering Selene's look.

"All right. Let's keep going."

They'd gotten to that point a couple times with other zodiacs. The real test began now.

"Okay, people. We'e going to the next stage. Increase beam power to our target value in a discontinuous frequency. I want an escape route if things go south."

"Copy that, operator. Discontinuous frequency established. Fire scale increasing by five...seven...nine percent and counting."

The beam of light was broken up into several pulses of energy shooting every few seconds.

"The force field holds." The technician ran a hand over his sweaty forehead. "Structural integrity at sixty-five percent. Biometric values are still in the green..."

"...Fire scale at ten percent of target value and counting," another voice added. "Nine...seven... Target at five percent!"

The room suddenly became quiet. Never had they come so close to their objective.

Selene activated her interlink. "Deborah? Talk to me."

She heard static, but no answer.

"Deborah?"

"Target at three percent of—"

"Bios." Selene cut her off. "What's her status?"

"She's still within the safety zone, operator. There aren't any discrepancies I can see."

Selene looked at the zodiac, standing perfectly still on the other side of the shatterproof glass. "Deborah? Can you hear me?"

"...two percent of the target!"

Selene bit her lip. Something was off. She turned to her right. "Control, abort the test."

The man behind the control station blinked. "Ma'am?"

"I said abort the—"

A scream pierced through her interlink. She turned just in time to see a burst of light coming from the test room.

"Shit!" Selene threw her visor to the ground, her eyes wild and unfocused. "Status report?"

"Force field out of phase, operator. Bios are out of sync. The zodiac is unconscious. Her right shoulder strap and the lower cannon are completely out of juice. I think...I think there's been a short circuit."

"Operator," called another technician. "The exosuit is leaking a dangerous quantity of carbon monoxide, nitrogen dioxide, and... Ma'am?"

Selene grabbed two masks and rushed toward the door.

"Ma'am!" The technician grabbed her arm. "We must wait for the rescue team. The fumes could—"

"Get the fuck out of my way!"

Selene pushed past the man, put on the mask, and entered the test room. A blast of hot air hit her like an invisible avalanche. She blinked, disoriented for a few seconds. It was hard to see a meter away. The smoke was everywhere.

"Deborah? Come in." She tried the interlink. "Can you hear me?"

Selene groped around until she found the girl lying on the floor. "Deborah?" She felt her pulse. "It's all right. I'm right here."

The air purifiers absorbed enough smoke to allow Selene to see better.

There was a large pool of blood all around Deborah. The shoulder strap and the lower right cannon were completely blackened. The helmet was gone. Selene couldn't see where it was.

"Christ." The force coil on both pieces of the armor had exploded, taking a piece of her arm with it. She pressed the mask on the zodiac's face. "Medic!" she cried out. "I need a medic!"

A squad of people in yellow overalls rushed inside the room a minute later.

"Remove the right side of the armor," Selene spoke quickly, glancing toward the bloody mess in front of her, "but leave the rest of the exosuit where it is. It's the only reason she is still alive."

"We'll do that."

They put Deborah on a stretcher and rushed her out.

Selene remained on her knees for a minute, concentrating only on her breathing. Slowly, she got to her feet and walked back into the control room. She pointed at one technician. "Do we have the data?"

"Yes, ma'am."

"Good." Selene's legs gave way, and she slumped on the first chair she could find. "I want to be updated on the zodiac's status. Everything that happens to her, I want to be the first one to know."

"Understood."

"And call the reserves. We're going to need a new zodiac when we figure out what the fuck went wrong. That's all. You are dismissed. All of you."

"Ma'am." One of the technicians cleared his throat and took a step forward. "Wei requested a post-operative report as soon as—"

"I said get out!"

The man recoiled, and the room grew quiet. Then, one by one, the team members left the room.

When the door was closed, Selene ran a shaky hand through her hair. "*You* fucked up," she said to the empty room. "They're not the ones you should be pissed at."

She took a blue pill from her breast pocket and swallowed it dry. Her muscles relaxed and her heartbeat slowed down in a matter of seconds.

She breathed in and out, her eyes shut.

This was the third accident in a week.

They should have never gotten to the testing phase so quickly. It was reckless. If it were up to her, she'd drop everything and go back to the design phase. But that wasn't possible if she wanted to stick to Wei's schedule.

"EVE?" Selene called out. Her voice was slow and tired.

"Yes, Selene?" a mechanical voice answered.

"What do you think it was this time? The intrasynaptic connection? Or do we have a purely mechanical problem?"

"It is hard to tell with the current data. Judging by the status of the force field just before the accident, there could be an issue in the synthetic connection between the undercut and the armor."

"Right. That's what I feared." Selene pushed herself up. "Send me all the data we gathered on the QUOD1 station. We need to work with what we have."

"Commencing transfer."

Selene rolled up her sleeves and began the long and tedious task of analyzing the post-op data. She spent the next hours looking at dozens of files and running diagnostics and simulations to prepare for the next test. When she glanced out the window, the sky was a dark mantle filled with stars.

She felt tired, ready to sink into bed and pass out. Had there really been a time when she'd looked forward to waking up in this godforsaken place?

That life seemed to belong to another person, someone more naive. A dreamer who deserved a kick in the teeth.

There will be a price to pay if you continue to work in Valhalla.

Wei had been right. She couldn't even blame him. It was her fault she was in that situation.

Beep. Beep. Beep.

Selene accepted the call. "Yes?"

"I heard you gave the team the rest of the day off." Birger's voice was even, but Selene had known him long enough to understand when he was worried.

"They needed some fresh air," Selene said. "So did I."

"I see." After a brief pause, her liaison asked, "How are you doing?"

"Splendid. Just trying to pick up the pieces and see what went wrong. How about you?"

"Same old. I wanted to update you on the zodiac's situation."

Selene sat down. "Okay. Go on."

"The medical team stopped the bleeding and stabilized her. They're confident she'll be out of danger soon."

"What about her arm?"

Birger's pause was longer this time. "I'm afraid she's going to lose it."

Selene clenched her hands into fists.

"Doctor? You still there?"

"I heard you." Selene swallowed hard. "Anything else?"

"Yes, actually. Wei requested the post-op report. He seemed eager to know what happened."

Selene rose from the chair. "Right," she said, striding out of the room. "Tell him it's on its way."

THE DOOR to Wei's quarters opened automatically.

She passed the hallway area and found Wei sitting in

front of a huge window-wall. His eyes were fixed on the night sky.

Selene looked around. There were clothes scattered on the floor, and cartons of Chinese food abandoned all over the place.

The apartment smelled of sweet and sour sauce and rotten meat.

"I've heard about the accident." The Genius Boy's voice was stark, devoid of any emotion. "Fill me in."

"The energy coil in the bracelet plate exploded," Selene said in little more than a whisper. "A fault in the original design of the suit. The part didn't match the overall energy level."

"Anything we could have done to avoid it?"

"Sure." Selene was fighting not to scream. "We could have *not* pushed the testing so soon. There's that."

Wei didn't seem bothered by the anger in her voice. He was still staring outside, his eyes glassy. "How's the zodiac?" he asked.

"She lost her arm."

Wei nodded, then looked back at the sky. "I understand. I'll take care of that."

Selene grabbed the back of a chair and squeezed the wood until she heard it creak.

I'll take care of that.

She'd heard him say these words at least a dozen times. The way he pronounced them felt inhuman, like he was sweeping the entrance to a patio door: a mundane action of negligible importance.

Son of a bitch.

"How can you do it?" Selene said, fingernails biting into her palms. "How do you keep that poker face after what I've said? At least *pretend* you give a damn."

"Are you here for another of your sermons?"

"I'm here for a goddamn answer, asshole."

"The hardest choices require this poker face, Selene. You should know this."

"Bullshit!" Selene slammed the chair on the floor. "You're sitting here, on top of your crystal tower, demanding *reports* and pontificating about the future of humanity, but you don't know what's happening out there."

Wei turned to look at her. "Rapid breathing, dilated pupils, pale skin, sweating forehead, agitation. You're in shock, my friend. Sit down and take a deep breath."

"I almost lost another person today, Wei. When will this end? *When*?"

"When we have a functional Seien."

"You'll never have one if you don't slow down. You're asking us to jump from a goddamned cliff and sprout wings as we're falling. It's not going to happen."

"I told you it wouldn't be easy."

"And you were goddamned right!" Selene clapped her hands mockingly. "I should have listened to you instead of getting deeper inside this fucking circus."

"Selene—"

"Did you happen to invent a time machine? Hmm? I'll take it. I'll take it and go punch my past self in the face..."

"Selene—"

"...and go back inside the fucking hole you found me in!"

"You're one of the brightest people I know."

Selene blinked. "What?"

"You are. You stuck with me for longer than I thought possible. I've thrown at you the most difficult tasks, the most insurmountable problems, and you did the impossible to solve them. Few people have given me more than you did.

You've earned my respect and trust. I understand your frustration, but we can't stop now. We're close to the finish line."

Selene shook her head. "You don't see it, do you?"

"I don't see what?"

"You're blind, Wei. You're lost inside your impossible, ideal world. That exosuit is a time bomb. We almost lost three zodiacs in the past seven days. Eight more will carry the consequences of their injuries for the rest of their lives. We can't go on like this. It's too risky. We need to go back to the design phase."

"No," Wei said. "We must move on."

"It's human lives we're talking about, you cold-blooded piece of shit!"

"I need those Seiens up and running."

"No shit! You made that plain enough. Why the hurry?"

"They're my insurance policy."

Selene frowned. "Insurance policy?"

"Yes."

"That's it? That's all you've got to say? I've spent three and a half years at your side, like a dog wagging its tail, doing everything you asked me to do. And now all you give me when I ask you a question is a fucking metaphor?"

"It's complicated."

"Then make it simple!"

"I wish that were possible."

"You don't trust me."

"I do trust you."

Selene forced a laugh. "Then talk to me. You owe me that much."

"I can't risk the safety of—"

"Oh, screw it!" Selene crossed her arms. "Don't feed me that bullshit. You're not looking after my safety, you're just keeping me in the dark because that's how your fucked-up mind works. You trust me? Prove it. Tell me why you need the Seien."

"Keeping you in the dark isn't a punishment, Selene. It's a blessing."

"Yeah? Tell it to the girl who's gonna wake up without a fucking arm!"

Wei sighed. He took a small container from his pocket, opened it, and took out a pill.

Selene snatched the drug box from Wei's hands. "Diteroxin?" Her eyes narrowed. "How long have you been taking this shit?"

"I can't waste a third of the day sleeping. There's too much to do."

"Really? That's a beautiful phrase to engrave on your tombstone, idiot. When was the last time you slept?"

"Irrelevant."

"Oh yeah? Think you can go around and ignore basic body needs? What will be next? You'll stop eating and shitting? You'll try to walk on water? Jesus, Wei. No wonder you look like a goddamn zombie. I don't give a damn what the others say about you. You're not a god."

"You're right. I'm just the Omnilogos." Wei cast his eyes down, looked at his empty hands. "It'll have to be enough."

"What the hell is that supposed to mean?"

"If I could give up more than my sleep, I would. There's too much at stake."

Selene wanted to hit him. She wanted it badly. But then Wei collapsed on the chair with a pathetic sigh, and he suddenly looked smaller and frail.

Depleted wasn't the right word, but it was close enough.

Selene's rage subsided, and she noticed the deep shadows besieging his eyes, his pale skin, his sluggish posture, as if his own body had become too heavy to carry.

"Wei," Selene exhaled through her teeth. "I'm worried about you. I want to help."

"You're already helping."

"You, *idiot*. I want to help *you*."

"Okay." Wei nodded absently. "Can you reverse time?"

"What?"

"Can you unmake choices I made years ago?"

"Wei. I don't—"

"Can you make me smarter? More cunning? Can you avoid all the mistakes I made when I thought nothing could stop me?"

"No," Selene said, looking at him with guilt. "No, I can't."

"Then you can only help me by completing Project Valhalla. Can you do that?"

"I don't know." Selene's voice was stretched, and she felt as tired as she must have looked. "Maybe. I just think the price to pay to speed things up is too high."

"Believe me, it's not."

"You're not going to tell me what scares you so much, are you?"

Wei opened his mouth, then closed it. He went back to look at the stars.

Selene cursed, then dragged a chair and sat across from him. "Do you enjoy making my life a living hell?"

"Actually, I'm doing everything I can to make it easier."

Selene smiled. "Wei, you're the smartest idiot I know."

"That's the kindest thing anyone has said to me today."

"I want to strangle you."

"You'll have to get in line."

Selene chuckled, a hollow sound that was short-lived. The room grew quiet.

"Did you know there are more planets in the universe than grains of sand in the Red Desert?"

Selene looked out of the window. "How can you be so sure? Did you count them?"

"I don't need to. I've got science on my side."

"Okay, well. Since you worship that word, it's also *scientifically* proven that if you stop sleeping, you die. What do you have to say about that?"

"You're being melodramatic."

"And you're being an asshole."

"Maybe." Wei nodded, as if seriously considering Selene's statement. "It's hard to know who I really am. However, what I want... Well, that's a hell of a lot clearer. And that's the only thing that matters."

Selene stared at him for a long minute, then smiled despite herself. *That* was what made Wei so different from anyone else. He could make you want to punch him, and yet you could listen to him talking for hours. It was the way he looked into your eyes, as if he could see your naked soul.

Birger was right. He made you believe that anything was possible.

"I need your help." Wei wet his lips. "I have a deadline to meet."

Selene frowned. "Another one?"

"Yes. I need the exosuit up and running before March."

"March? Are you out of your mind? That's less than three months from now!"

"The universe was formed in a week."

"Well, if I meet God, I'll ask him how he did it. In the meantime, you can't expect miracles from a puny human being."

"Maybe God didn't create the universe," Wei said. "Maybe it was someone hard-pressed to meet a deadline."

"Did you hear anything I said? About the accident? I'm

already struggling to keep up with your schedule. Now you're asking me to speed things up further?"

"I believe you can do it."

Selene tried very hard not to scream. "Listen," she said, "I'd give you the Moon if I could. But this is just too much. We've just barely kept a stable connection between the zodiac and the Seien. I need more time to generate a reliable K.T. field. I can't give you a functioning Seien by March. It's impossible."

"The impossible is only a possibility that has not yet been discovered."

"Yeah, sure. That's a hell of a catchphrase. Maybe I'll have it tattooed on my forearm."

"Selene—"

"However," she cut him off, her voice sharp, "it doesn't change the hard, cold truth. You know? The place where normal people live? The one subject to the laws of physics? We're already sending half a dozen people a month to the infirmary. If we speed things up further, we might as well start digging graves."

"That's a risk I'm willing to take."

Selene looked into his eyes; two amber braziers with the strength of two stars. "Why are you taking these risks, Wei? What scares you so much? Tell me, *please*."

"You don't have to know. Knowing is *my* prerogative, my burden." Wei stood up from the chair. "You have three months."

"What happens in three months?"

Wei threw the Diteroxin into the garbage bin.

"Wei?"

The Genius Boy looked at her as if he saw her for the first time. "In three months, the world will change forever."

7

AUDERE

(THREE MONTHS LATER)

Polaris. The most complex, expensive, and daring project in the history of humankind had been revealed.

Fucking Wei Wang. Just when she thought he couldn't surprise her anymore, he pulled out another ace from his ass.

Selene couldn't keep the smile off her face. Wei managed to keep the greatest infrastructure project in history hidden for years. In the Information Age.

Selene turned off the screen and rubbed her forehead. She felt a headache slowly building.

She'd watched Wei's presentation broadcasted by Worldview three times already, and was still trying to wrap her head around it.

Hyperist. It was the word Wei used to describe a political and social movement aimed at creating a spacefaring civilization.

It was the first time Selene had heard the word and knew it would set the ether on fire.

Wei's slogan—"From stardust to stardust"—had turned

into a catchphrase, spreading into cyberspace at light speed. However, the media showed that the public opinion was divided about Polaris. People either hated the idea or revered it. Right or wrong. Black or white. There were no shades of gray.

People wanted to know how on earth Wei had kept something this massive a secret. For once, Selene had the answer.

Years before, Birger told her that Wei was building centers like Valhalla all over the world. Selene was sure he'd used the same information-containing system used in Valhalla. That was why Polaris had remained hidden until the end. Each floor must have worked on a separate component of Polaris, knowing nothing about what other floors were doing. It was a brilliant way of keeping everyone in the dark while the project was completed.

Selene wondered how many other Valhallas were out there. How many projects was Wei developing in the shadow?

Questions that Wei probably would never answer.

There were important implications for Polaris. Its impact on public opinion was clear: it turned Wei into a target.

Douglas Woodside wanted his head, for starters. Groups of Landists had surrounded government institutions all over the world to demand the construction of Polaris be stopped.

The war to win public opinion had already begun, and Selene knew exactly what side she was fighting for.

Her interlink signaled an incoming call. She accepted it.

"We're ready, Doctor."

"I'm on my way."

Selene headed for the exit. Her time had come; her turn to make history.

FOUR ZODIACS WERE STANDING in front of as many fire mouths. Each Seien glowed with a pale aquamarine light; a signal the exosuits were powered on and ready to go.

It was the day of the deadline. Today, everything was on the line. The four people on the other side of the shatter-proof glass were going to make history or die trying.

"Operator?"

Selene turned to the stuff member who called her.

"All stations are standing by."

"Copy that, systems," Selene said. "Commence countdown."

"Yes, ma'am."

The unveiling of Polaris revealed something important to Selene. Wei had become a target. She was sure the Seiens would become a way of protecting him, and God only knew the kid was going to need protection. She now knew why Project Valhalla existed, and this knowledge gave her purpose.

"...Three...two...one..."

"Fire!"

Beams of light erupted from the fire mouths and shattered on the exosuit's force fields in a matter of seconds.

Selene read the data as half a dozen voices fed her information.

"Increase firepower by fifty percent," she ordered.

The beam of light intensified, and the zodiacs strengthened their shields accordingly. Once again, the light beam bounced against the force fields.

This is it. This is when everything we worked on can blow up in our face big time.

All eyes turned to her.

She inhaled sharply. "Weaponry, turn up the juice to maximum power following pattern Omega 66. Let's make them sweat."

"Roger that, operator. Fire mouth's energy increasing to one hundred percent."

The cannons fired stronger beams against the zodiacs. Their barriers held, but this time they couldn't break the energy beams. They could barely fend them off.

"Intensity increasing ten...twenty...thirty percent."

"The force fields show signs of destabilization," said the system technician. "Structural integrity at fifty-five percent and falling. The K.T. field is compensating, but weakening rapidly..."

"...Fire scale at eighty percent of target," another voice from the back of the room shouted. "Eighty-nine... Ninety-two... Target at ninety-five percent!"

A piercing sound flooded the control room.

"Shut down the proximity alarm," Selene ordered.

"Copy that, operator."

The noise stopped abruptly.

"Bios? Give me a reading."

"Sigyn's bios are rapidly deteriorating. Pressure in her exosuit is rising. She might pass out any moment, ma'am."

"Loki, Odin." Selene looked at the two zodiacs on the far right of the testing room. "Take some of the heat off Sigyn's back, will you?"

"Roger that, Doc," came two voices in unison.

"Jarsir?" Selene looked at the remaining zodiac. "Send a synaptic burst into Sigyn's matrix. We need to keep her awake. I need all four of you for the fireworks. Can't afford to lose her."

"Copy that, Doc. SB sent."

Selene looked at Sigyn. The zodiac was shaking her head, then she straightened.

"Sigyn?" Selene called. "You're with us?"

The Zodiac raised her thumb. "Sorry about that, Doc. I'm fine. My telemetry wasn't working. I was getting cooked. Am I still in the game?"

"Definitely. I'm betting Loki and Odin would love you to help them out with the heat. What do you say?"

"I'm all for it."

Selene raised her hand. "Go on, Falsia. Give it more gas."

"Ninety-seven percent fire scale—"

"—and structural integrity of the—"

"—biometric values—"

"—ninety-eight percent and counting—"

Numbers, graphs, statistics. Selene could see the big picture. The puzzle was no longer a puzzle. It was a language she understood well because it was *her* language.

Selene pushed a button on her console. "Signal them to twin."

"Order sent, operator."

"Target reached!"

The moment the plasma beam turned fiery red, the zodiacs' energy bubbles became a single force field that included all four of them. The new barrier took on a white color, its outlines resembling a crystal dome. The new barrier broke the plasma beam in a second.

"Energy flow interrupted. The barrier held!"

A shout erupted in the control room. Hands were shaken and people exchanged big smiles.

Selene shook hands and returned the smiles of people who had worked on this program for years.

They were finally ready.

ALL OF VALHALLA'S resources were directed toward producing the first generation of fully operational Seiens. Wei had called the first batch of the new exosuits "Audere." *To dare*, in Latin.

The Genius Boy loved larger than life concepts.

Two months had passed since the successful testing of the Seiens, and fifty exosuits had been manufactured. A staggering number, considering all the resources that went into creating one.

Selene looked out the window of floor BIO. Rain battered against the iron-colored transports stationed a few hundred yards from Valhalla. A group of technicians were carrying large carbondurene boxes, each containing armor worth as much as a small airplane.

"Don't worry. Your children will be fine."

Selene turned. The Genius Boy had just stepped inside the room, the door closing behind him. He looked like he hadn't had a good night's sleep in the last year or two.

"You look like shit," she said.

Wei tipped an imaginary hat and smiled. "It's nice to see you too."

Selene glanced at the cup Wei was holding. "Espresso?"

"Yeah, the fourth of the day," he said, dark red circles around his eyes. "You want one?"

"I can't stand the smell."

"Oh, I see. Is the scent stirring old memories? Hmm? You, wearing a dangerously orange apron while smiling at customers, grinding coffee beans, and serving strawberry cheesecakes?"

"You want a punch in the face?"

"Hey, *you* made me quit the pills, remember?"

"Which, apparently, turned you into a caffeine addict."

"Oh well." Wei sipped the espresso. "I won't deny it. This stuff is worse than heroin."

The young man walked up to her, then looked out the window. Valhalla's personnel were loading the transports with the exosuits.

"You made me worry, you know?" Wei said. "Thought you might not meet the deadline."

"That makes two of us." Selene nodded toward the transports. "Birger said you're transporting them somewhere in the Yellow Sea."

Wei shrugged. "Maybe."

"I hope they're not a gift for your Chinese investors."

"Is that what's bothering you? Giving a military advantage to what's already the most powerful nation on the planet? Or are you trying to get me to talk?"

Selene pursed her lips. The smile was all in her eyes. "I tried."

Wei drank the last of his coffee, then set the cup on the table. "Valhalla is the forge of the Seiens. Now it's time to train the right people to make the best use of them."

"Something tells me you already found these people."

Wei bobbed his head. "You know I hate wasting time."

"How many?"

"Fifty, give or take. The number will go up in the next few months."

Selene crossed her arms. She suddenly felt very cold. "So, now that you have your super army, what are you going to do with it?"

"Honestly? I hope to do absolutely nothing with it."

Selene narrowed her eyes. "You've squeezed Valhalla's resources dry, spent billions of dollars and risked the lives of more people than I care to admit to do...what? Crack a joke?"

"I told you the exosuits were part of an insurance policy. Few people will get one hoping to use it, but when shit hits the fan, they can thank God they have one."

8

INFINITY

(2030)

This was the first time Selene witnessed an event that would go down in history.

The Infinity control center was a huge structure, dwarfing anything she had seen before. It was a tribute to everything Wei Wang had believed in all his life: to dare, to strive for something more, something better.

The Skyrise room—the biggest in the building and capable of seating ten thousand people—was the epicenter of the world, a stage that over three billion people were watching live from around the globe at that moment.

The space elevator had worked its magic. Polaris, the orbital wagon strapped to a 22,000-mile-long cable, had left Earth with no complication.

Wei Wang had made history once again.

The huge room filled with people was eerily quiet. Selene could feel her heartbeat quicken as she watched the audience stare at the stage: it was empty, for now.

She looked around. Among these people, there were heads of state, presidents of giant corporations, as well as several entertainment personalities. She had even glimpsed the media buff, Gosema Omen, and the world-famous eterion, Cantara Handal.

Well, Selene was neither a celebrity nor a woman of power, but she knew people. She had to cash in quite a few favors—accumulated by working for over six years in Valhalla—to get a ticket, but it was worth it. She wouldn't have missed this moment for the world.

"Are we ready, Joe?"

Selene turned to her right, where a reporter with a broad face was speaking to a cameraman in a harsh tone.

"Yes, boss. We're live in five, four, three, two, one..."

The reporter's annoyed expression turned into a wide smile. "Yes, Sasha," he said, nodding. "It's been a day. You can feel the electricity in the air. This is history in the making. Now that the five minutes of terror have passed, Wei Wang is expected in the press room to comment on the performance of the launch and answer questions."

The doors on the other side of the stage slowly opened. A figure emerged from the passage, followed by other people.

Selene stood up with the rest of the audience and began clapping.

"The door is opening," the reporter said, his forehead shiny with sweat. "Yes, there he is! Wei Wang is greeted with applause and a general standing ovation."

Selene recognized the members of Wei's inner circle, the Hexahedron, emerging from the doorway. Mark Strutzenberg, the CEO of Gaia, and Gladia Egea, the co-founder of SOL, were following Wei a few steps behind. After them came Toshio Shimao, chief researcher of Paragon Corporation, Patrick Trudeau, chief engineer of I & I, and Isaac Nazarov, the founder of Archetype Unlimited.

"Ladies and gentlemen." A mechanical voice rang

through the room. "We have the honor of welcoming Wei Wang, a visionary mind, the First Hyperist, the creator of the module Polaris, and the director of the project Space Zero."

Selene focused on Wei's emaciated face. It'd been over a year since she'd seen him in person. His visits to Valhalla had become rare and far in between. She missed his smug face, his cocky attitude. Valhalla just wasn't the same without him.

The Genius Boy's smile was the only thing she recognized. Wei had lost weight, deep shadows besieged his eyes, and he was showing signs of fatigue. Was he using Diteroxin again?

The applause subsided, and Selene and the rest of the spectators sat.

"To write history is a wonderful experience," Wei began, silencing the last few murmurs in the room. "It gives you a very special perspective on the world around you and helps you understand one very important thing: impossible is only a possibility that has not yet been discovered."

The general standing ovation that followed prevented Wei from continuing his speech. Twice he tried to resume, and twice he was interrupted by whistles and applause.

Selene clapped with the rest of the audience, a big smile on her face. This was the crowning achievement of everything Wei had worked for. All the sacrifices he'd made, the choices he'd taken, was because of this moment.

The applause finally died down, and Wei opened his mouth again.

A sudden explosion erupted from within the room, followed almost immediately by a wave of multicolored light.

Selene jumped up, looking around frantically as

screams pierced the room and a wave of panic washed over everyone.

"What the hell..."

Security drones emerged from hidden slots in the walls and dozens of men in uniform screamed.

"OUT, EVERYONE! GET THE HELL OUT OF HERE!"

The emergency doors opened in unison. Hundreds of people piled toward the exit; many fell and were trampled by the tide of people jostling to escape.

Selene remained motionless, her muscles frozen as she stared at the horror unfolding before her eyes. She turned toward the stage, her eyes wide.

Wei's face was devoid of any emotion. For a split second, their eyes met, and Selene opened her mouth to say something. A second explosion broke the world in two.

Wei was hit by a beam of light and thrown off the chair. He bumped violently against the wall and fell to the ground.

"No!" Selene ran toward the stage. "Wei!"

"An explosion, we think..." the reporter was yelling a million miles away, his voice broken by shouts and cries for help. "They're still shooting! Strutzenberg and Shimao... lying on the ground! They've been hit by something! I can't see... Almighty God!"

"WEI!"

Someone grasped her arm, causing her to turn. It was a man in uniform.

"Get out!" he shouted, his face flushed with anger. "Are you deaf?"

"No!" Selene punched him in the face. The man loosened his grip, but didn't let go. "I've got to help him!"

"I said *out*!"

Another explosion threw them both to the ground.

Selene's ears popped, and her vision became foggy. Vaguely, in the corners of her awareness, she heard a voice.

"The First Hyperist is being taken away by the medical team. We do not know the condition..."

Wei.

Selene struggled to get up.

She had to find Wei.

She had to help him.

She hobbled, pain rising from her spine. She didn't care. She kept moving. The deadly beams of light roared left and right, followed by a scream as people fell all around her. There was smoke spreading from one side of the room. It was hard to see.

I need to find him. I need to...

The stretcher passed her, just a few feet away. She froze on the spot. Wei lay on the stretcher, his eyes wide open, lifeless.

"No." Selene fell to the ground, hitting hard on her knees.

That wasn't possible.

It couldn't be.

She blinked her tears away.

Wei Wang couldn't be dead.

The world became a blur of images and sounds. She saw a man in the corner of her vision, tall and completely covered in a dark jumpsuit...or was it armor? She couldn't say. Everything was happening too fast. The man raised his right arm and then...something happened. The arm changed shape.

Selene gasped as she turned her head to stare at the impossible thing happening before her. The man's arm had transformed into a strange sort of appendix that looked like liquid metal. It became long and thin, shaped like a straight tube. A *barrel*. She was staring at a weapon.

Selene screamed a warning, but no one heard her.

The stranger shot someone with the same red beam that had hit Wei, and another person fell somewhere in the room.

Selene closed her eyes, even though she was forcing herself to keep them open. She wanted to see; she wanted to know. But her strength seeped out, and she lost her fight against oblivion.

9

SHADOWS

(ONE MONTH LATER)

Selene poured more whiskey in the glass, her eyes fixed on the prototype of the Seien Wei had shown her five years before.

Five years. Just the thought made her shiver. It seemed like five *million* years had passed.

She touched the smooth surface of the armor, hating every inch.

"What the fuck was the whole point?" Her voice was broken, unsteady. "He said you'd be his insurance policy. Then why the fuck did he die?"

Selene knocked back the amber-colored liquid, then refilled it with shaky hands.

Whoever had killed Wei was continuing the work started at Infinity. A few days after the attack, two of his closest collaborators, Trudeau and Nazarov, died in their homes. No one believed they committed suicide, as the evidence seemed to suggest.

Someone had murdered them.

Gladia Egea was the last member of the Hexahedron

still alive. Many believed it was only a matter of time before she, too, was killed.

"Doctor?"

Selene turned sharply. She hadn't noticed Birger entering the room.

"Yes?" She swallowed hard, feeling a sour taste in the back of her mouth.

"You didn't answer the interlink."

"I turned it off. What's up?"

"I have orders to transfer you to another facility."

Selene frowned. "Ordered by whom?"

"I'm afraid the information is classified."

"What's cooking? Why do I have to leave?"

"It's for your safety. All Wei's collaborators with your level of clearance to the Central Nodes are deemed sensible targets."

"Who gave the order?"

"It's—"

"Wait. Let me guess. It's classified."

Birger sighed. "Trust me. Valhalla is no longer safe. There's a shuttle waiting for you outside of the—"

Selene pointed to the exosuit. "Did you know he wore it?"

"I... What?"

"Wei. He wore this Seien. It's the earliest prototype. It's slow, imprecise, and as safe as a minefield. He wanted to show me what it could do. I remember that day like it was yesterday. I had been trying for a whole year to align the matrix core with the Interloop technology, and I failed big time. Without that connection, this power armor was just a very expensive bunch of metal. I went to his apartment that day and submitted my resignation. You know what he did? He tore the letter up the moment I gave it to him, saying...

Fuck, I still remember. He said: 'I will not become your biggest regret. Go back to work and stop wasting our time.'" She took a long sip from the glass, then shook her head. "That same day, he wore the Seien and said, 'Go ahead, test it on me.' Do you understand? He risked his own life to prove his stupid mantra: the impossible is just a possibility that hasn't been discovered."

"Doctor—"

"And now he's dead, Birger. Dead! Why? All our sacrifices, all that time wasted making this shit functional!" Selene kicked the armor twice, spilling the contents of her glass on the floor. "He never said it, but I know he made this suit to protect himself. I know he was expecting something. Well, it didn't matter. They got him, whoever 'they' are."

"Doctor Sato—"

"What I'm saying is that he failed! We all failed. This whole building, Project Valhalla, is a fucking joke."

"No, it's not."

Selene turned to look at the liaison. "What?"

"There's a lot more to the Seien than you think."

"What the hell are you talking about?"

"The armors were put to good use."

"Were they?" Selene walked up to him. "Go tell it to Wei's corpse!"

"You don't understand. Wei never wanted to protect himself. He didn't create the Seien for that reason."

"Then *why* the fuck did he create them?"

"To give us a chance."

"A...chance?" Selene stumbled on the word. "What chance?"

"Wei had a plan." Birger had a grim twist to his mouth; his pose was unnaturally still. "Valhalla was just the tip of the iceberg. There are other buildings like this, still working for his legacy. His project still needs people like you, Doctor. You can still make a difference if—"

The lights in the room went out, and for a moment, darkness surrounded them. Then the emergency LED turned on and cast an ominous red light all around.

"What's going on?" Selene asked.

Birger touched his wireless earpiece. "Staunch? Report." His face became more tense. "Understood. No, stay where you are. Destroy the data center. I'll bring her outside myself." He broke the connection and took Selene's arm. "We need to go."

"You wanna tell me what the hell—"

"We're under attack."

Selene's eyes went wide. "What? Under attack?"

An explosion hurled them to the ground.

"Shit." Pieces of the ceiling fell around Selene.

"Get up!" Birger helped her to her feet. "We need to keep moving. This way."

They ran down the corridor, heading for the fire escape as the corridor's floor shook under their feet. The smell of smoke was thick in the air.

Selene heard more explosions and screams in the distance. Someone was shooting. She stared in horror at a pair of bodies lying on the ground, crushed by metal beams.

"Birger! We need to help them."

"They're gone. Keep moving!"

Valhalla had turned into a kill zone. The further they walked, the more bodies they found. The acrid smell of smoke followed them everywhere. Selene coughed.

"Put your head down, Doctor."

Something pressed against her face. It was a mask.

"Breathe," she heard Birger's voice over the growing clamor. "Slowly and steady. You have to—"

Another explosion swallowed the rest of Birger's sentence. Selene was thrown to the side of the corridor and a blaze of pain pierced her leg. The pain was so sharp and sudden, it left her breathless. She clenched her teeth and touched her leg. A metal splinter the size of her thumb stuck from her quadriceps.

"Doctor? Are you okay?"

"My leg," she murmured, in shock. "Can't... I can't move it."

Birger took her under his arm. "Hold on. Lean on me."

The liaison led her up the stairs, half carrying her.

They arrived on a landing badly lit by emergency lights.

"Hang in there. We're almost out."

After an eternity, Selene glimpsed the outline of an archway. Birger entered a code on the panel and a piece of the wall slid to the side, revealing an exit. A blast of freezing air hit them. Birger pushed her out.

The night was cold, the sky a succession of everlasting lights.

"There's a shuttle waiting for us outside," the liaison said, drawing his gun.

Selene trudged forward, pain radiating from her leg like a snake's bite. "Who...who's attacking?"

"Just keep walking."

Selene gritted her teeth and continued to drag herself forward. Every step felt like a metal rod stabbing through her leg.

In the distance, she saw a hill with something faintly reflecting the moonlight. She recognized an Ulur class shuttle: the cockpit shaped like a falcon's beak, and the main body built like a huge egg pressed on both sides.

"Yes, Staunch," Birger spoke quickly, his voice raspy between coughs. "She's with me. Have you warned the governor? Good. Start the engines. No. We can't wait for—"

A roar ripped through the silence of the night.

Selene turned just in time to see a beam of light cut the sky in half before it fell over the top of the hill with a mighty crash. The shockwave threw Selene to the ground. She tasted blood in her mouth, and the world became a collection of shapes blurred into a confusion of colors.

"Shit! B...Birger?" she groaned, trying to turn her head to see around. It took her a couple minutes before the world came back into focus. She squinted, trying to make sense of the mess of light and shapes in front of her. The shuttle had been reduced to pieces. What remained of the hull was scattered all over the hillside.

"Birger!" She looked for the liaison, but couldn't find him. "Birger, are you—" She cut herself off as something caught her eye. Two men were walking through the rubble. They were tall, both dressed in dark jumpsuits that covered them head to toe. Selene blinked. Or maybe not. Maybe that wasn't a jumpsuit. There was something strange in the way their bodies reflected the moonlight, as if whatever covered them was made out of metal. She blinked again. Maybe she'd smashed her head too hard.

A scream ripe with pain came from the hill's crest. Selene shifted her gaze in that direction. The pilot of the shuttle had somehow survived the attack. He was crawling out of the wreckage.

The two strangers caught up with him. One of them pinned him down by pushing a foot on his back. The other attacker raised an arm and...it changed shape, then opened up like the petals of a huge flower. A beam of light struck the pilot, and Selene screamed.

Flashes of images exploded before her eyes, like the left-over of a nightmare she couldn't get rid of.

A vision of the Polaris attack played out all over again. Hundreds of people scrambling toward the exit. Bodies lying on the ground, eyes open, lifeless.

Those two were the same people who had attacked the Infinity Center, the terrorists who killed Wei and almost all his collaborators.

And they had come to finish the job.

The attackers turned and walked toward Selene. As they got closer, Selene could see them better. Their eyes were long and thin, bright orange in the darkness of the night.

"Shit."

Selene moved in the opposite direction as fast as she could, but her legs wouldn't respond. She dragged herself across the ground, then a hand grabbed her hair and pulled her up. She cried out in pain.

"She's alive, Alpha." The attacker had a sharp, metallic voice. It didn't seem to belong to a person.

From up close, Selene saw black scales covered their faces, like a grotesque approximation of a reptilian man. And not just on the face. The same otherworldly thing covered their whole body. She realized *that* was their skin.

"Identify her, Karabu."

The reptilian man studied her for a second. "Selene Sato," he said. "Head researcher of the Valhalla Project. Class one target."

"Take her," said the leader. "The Archetype could use her."

"Yes, Alpha."

The one called Karabu grabbed Selene with his other hand, then stopped.

"What is it?"

"I'm picking up gravimetric signals coming from the northeast."

"Dunamis?" Alpha looked up at the sky. "Impossible. Ariul is too far away."

"Confirmed," Karabu said. "It's them."

"How many?"

"A squadron. Fifty. Maybe more."

The leader looked to the northeast. Magma-colored eyes narrowed to slits.

"They're getting closer, Alpha."

Selene sensed the apprehension in his tone.

"Gather the others." Alpha looked away and stepped back. "We have no orders to engage the enemy."

Karabu pointed toward Selene. "What about her?"

Alpha tossed her a glance. "Finish her."

Karabu looked at Selene with a blank expression. His arm morphed into the flower-shaped gun that killed the pilot, and Selene felt the heat of the weapon as it charged.

A gunshot ripped through the silence, and the beam of light meant to end her missed her by a whisker.

Alpha's body hit the ground hard. In place of his left eye, there was a big burning hole.

Karabu stepped back. The scales on his forehead clustered in the center of his face in what looked like an expression of astonishment.

Selene turned around sharply. Birger was holding the gun with both hands, his face covered in blood.

"Run!" he shouted to Selene.

The liaison fired another half-dozen rounds in quick succession, but he had lost the element of surprise.

Karabu sprinted forward, his arm turning into a black blade as he charged Birger. He struck the liaison in the chest, burying his arm deep into the man.

Birger spat blood and fell first on his knees, then on his back. He didn't move again.

"No!"

Karabu's arm turned into the nightmarish shotgun weapon and pointed it at Selene. "Receive the blessing of the Light," he said.

Selene covered her eyes from the blinding light, waiting for the end.

There was a sudden roar, followed by a dull noise, like something heavy dropping on the ground. When Selene opened her eyes again, a figure shrouded in light stood between her and the monster.

Selene gaped as she recognizing the familiar glow radiating from the power armor she helped create.

A woman was wearing a sunset-colored Seien. And not just any Seien. It was one of the first Audere-class exosuits Valhalla had produced two years back.

"Hellhound intercepted, Governor," said the newcomer, looking at Karabu.

"Roger that, Felicity," answered a voice interspersed with static. "Leave something for the others."

"Can't make any promises, sir."

Karabu growled. His left arm morphed into a sword-like weapon.

"Your friends are far away," the scaly being said, nodding to the sky. "I can kill you a dozen times before they get here."

"I can kill you once, and that'll be enough."

Karabu fired a beam of light...which shattered against the force field created by the exosuit.

Felicity raised her arm, and from the end of the vambrace came an energy saber. "Do your worst, pretty face."

Karabu threw himself against her and the two began an all-out battle.

One thing was clear to Selene. The woman who came to her rescue was no ordinary zodiac. Her movements were quick and precise, as if she'd done nothing but use the power armor for years. She was wearing it like a second skin.

It was exactly as Wei had envisioned it.

Regardless, the monster wasn't overcome. His speed and strength were superhuman, and matched the woman's attacks blow by blow.

Selene began searching for Birger's gun, but the growing darkness made it difficult to see where it might be on the frozen ground.

"Brother."

Selene turned as a new mechanical voice spoke.

A black figure descended from the sky, followed by a second and a third.

Karabu's face broke into a smile. "I thought you were gone. Alpha ordered you to fall back."

"We don't leave a brother behind."

The other three raised their arms, ready to fire.

"Governor?" Felicity touched the side of her helmet as she stepped back. "I could really use the cavalry now."

"They're almost there," a voice answered.

"There's one 'almost' too many in that sentence."

The monsters fired a rapid succession of light beams at Felicity. A couple of them hit the exosuit, and the armor was completely blackened where it absorbed the blow.

"Shit!" Felicity gritted her teeth as she slumped to the ground. "I've been hit! I repeat, I've been..."

Felicity never saw Karabu's shot coming. She collapsed to the ground, and her Seien stopped glowing.

The scaly being grabbed her by the helmet. "Now I'm going to enjoy watching you die."

Selene's hand brushed against a piece of metal on the ground. *Found*! She grabbed the weapon and fired at the demon's face.

Karabu fell to the ground, and Felicity collapsed on top of him.

The other three monsters turned toward Selene. They hadn't noticed her until that moment.

One of them shoved her before she could shoot again, and the gun fell to the ground.

Selene blinked, the pain coursing through her body almost unbearable. She didn't even have enough strength to scream.

A blinding light came from above.

Half a dozen people wearing Seiens formed a circle around their fallen comrades, the glow of the exosuits lighting the surroundings.

"Captain, are you all right?" asked one newcomer, a tall man donning a cyan-colored exosuit.

"Yeah," Felicity groaned. "I'll live, I think. Don't thank me all at once. I kept them warm for you."

"Very kind of you, Captain."

The battle ended quickly.

The bodies of the four monsters lay on the ground, charred and still. All dead.

Selene put her head on the icy ground. She struggled to breathe.

"Confirmed, Governor," said one soldier. "All hell-hounds have been neutralized. The Slayer will never know what happened to her abominations. The fortress is secure."

Felicity stood up with the help of one of her companions. "Rico, cover sector three. I want to know if there are any more coming."

"Roger that, Captain."

"We found another group of technicians in the rubble cap," said one soldier. "All dead. Are there any survivors there?"

Felicity pointed to Selene. "Just one."

"Is she still alive?"

"I hope so. She saved my life. Go give her a look."

Selene felt something cold placed over her forehead.

"Barely," said a voice. "Internal bleeding, and more broken bones than I can count. I don't think she's gonna make it, Cap."

"Take her to the Falcon. Inform the governor that we'll arrive with a guest."

"Yes, ma'am."

Selene felt a tingle in her neck. Then the world plunged into darkness.

10

ALCAZAR

(ONE WEEK LATER)

Beep. Beep. Beep.

A drop of sound in the echo of her mind.

She was falling. Selene was falling faster and faster.

She'd never awake again. That was the end.

She saw a blinding light, followed by an explosion.

Then nothing.

~

Beep. Beep. Beep.

That sound again.

Constant. Insistent. Annoying like a mosquito you can't see.

Selene found herself in a limbo of noises, memories, and sensations she could not get away from.

She was trapped, imprisoned in her own mind.

Beep. Beep. Beep.

That was the sound of her prison before oblivion flooded everything again.

"DOCTOR SATO?"

A voice at the edge of her consciousness.

Was she dreaming?

Please. No more nightmares.

"Doctor Sato? Can you hear me?"

Slowly, she opened her eyes.

It was like being born a second time.

It took a minute for her eyes to adjust to the light. She was in a large room with dull green walls and a pearl-white floor.

"Ah. Glad you're back."

Selene turned her head just enough to see the man sitting to her right.

He had a long aquiline nose and brown skin, like someone who had spent too much time under the sun. Selene tried to open her mouth, but felt a suffocating pressure on her chest that made it hard to breathe.

Pain. So much pain. She gasped, a wave of panic crashing on her like the hammer of a vengeful god.

"Don't strain yourself," the stranger said, placing a reassuring hand on her shoulder. "You can't talk just yet. The good news is, you'll be up and about in no time. The worst is behind you."

Selene noticed another person standing on the other side of the room. A woman dressed in a lab coat. A hospital. This must be a hospital.

"My name is Alcazar," the dark-skinned man said. "I knew Wei."

Selene stared at him, her jaw clenched tight.

"He told me a lot about you. I've tried to arrange your transportation as soon as possible, but there have been...

unforeseeable circumstances that delayed me." He sighed, then shook his head. "I'm sorry about what happened. Just know that now you're safe."

Selene swallowed, then tried to speak but only whimpered something incomprehensible.

"Sir?"

Alcazar turned toward the woman with the lab coat. He inhaled sharply, then bobbed his head once.

Selene felt something stinging her shoulder, then a sudden weariness washed over her.

"Rest," Alcazar said, as the room started fading away into the background. "We'll talk more when you wake up."

WHEN SHE OPENED her eyes again, the crushing weight on her chest was gone.

The man with the long nose was by her side. "Are you feeling better?" he asked.

Selene blinked, trying to put things together. She remembered fragments of what he said the last time, but couldn't remember his name.

"Do you remember me?"

Alcazar. His name was Alcazar.

Selene nodded.

"Drink this." Alcazar handed her a plastic cup with a straw. "It's a saline solution with electrolytes, potassium, and magnesium. It'll make you feel better. After you drink, you can try to talk. It should go better than the first time."

Selene took the glass, drank some of the content, and then cleared her throat. "Where..." She swallowed, then tried again. "Where are we?"

"North of the Barents Sea," Alcazar said. "I realize it's not much of an answer, but it'll have to be enough for now."

"The others?" Selene bit the inside of her cheek. "Where are the people...the other people living at Valhalla?"

"I'm afraid you are the only survivor of the Valhalla Center."

The only survivor.

Reality hit her like a brick. So that hadn't been a nightmare.

"You..." Selene blinked slowly. "Who are you?"

"Someone who should have acted faster, instead of burying his head in the sand."

Selene looked at her legs, only then realizing she couldn't feel anything below her waist. "I...I can't feel my legs."

Alcazar's expression turned sour. "You have suffered heavy injuries, Dr. Sato. It's a miracle you're alive."

"Will I... Will I be able to walk?"

"In time, yes, you might. But it's a long while away."

Alcazar nodded toward the left side of the room. She followed his gaze and saw a wheelchair. A chill ran down her spine. Her fear must have showed on her face because when Alcazar spoke, his face was kinder.

"I know what it feels like." The man picked up something from the floor and showed it to her. It was a walking cane. "I can't walk without this. Something I've learned to live with since I was a teenager. You'll get used to it."

Selene exhaled slowly. "You said you knew Wei."

"Yes."

"Is he really dead?"

Alcazar tapped his cane on the floor. "I'm afraid so."

"What about Valhalla? Who attacked us? I saw people wearing...wearing power suits to fight those monsters."

Alcazar raised an eyebrow. "Yes. They were wearing your

Seiens. You remember a lot more than I expected."

"You know about the Seiens?"

"I do."

"Did Wei create the exosuit... Did he create them to fight those monsters?"

Alcazar crossed his arms. "The simple answer is yes. He wanted a way to fight them."

"Who are *them*?"

"That, Doctor, is a *very* long story."

"I've no plans for the rest of the day."

Alcazar's smile was barely a stretch of his lips. "Let's make a deal," he said.

"What deal?"

"I run a project very much like Valhalla. When you recover, I'll give you a choice. You can return to your civilian life, or join us. We need brilliant minds, now more than ever. And if you wish, you can continue to make a difference by working on my project."

"Project? What project?"

"One that makes your exosuit look like a walk in the park."

Selene stared into the man's brown eyes. "You joking?"

"No reason to. My project is bigger, more complicated, and more meaningful than anything you've worked on before."

Something surfaced in Selene's mind. "Wait a second. Are you the one they called the Governor?"

Alcazar appraised for a long moment before saying, "Yes, I am called the Governor."

"Governor of what?"

"Of nothing, yet."

"I don't understand."

"I told you it was complicated."

Selene studied her savior. He couldn't have been more than thirty years old. There was nothing remarkable about his appearance, yet the intensity in those eyes reminded her of someone else's.

No. He looked nothing like him.

"Your part in the Seien project is over," Alcazar said, "but your knowledge of subjects like force fields, advanced inter-link synergy, and long-wave resonance fields is unmatched in the world. It would be an honor if you'd decide to work with us."

"*Us?*" Selene brought a shaky hand to her forehead. "Who's us?"

A weary smile flashed on Alcazar's face. "At the risk of sounding melodramatic, Doctor, we are humanity's last hope."

The end

If you liked *Project Valhalla*, please be awesome and review it on Amazon. Thanks!

REVIEW PROJECT VALHALLA ON AMAZON

CONTINUE THE SERIES...

Legacy of Ariul, the second book in The Omnilogos Singularity series, is now available on Amazon!

GET LEGACY OF ARIUL

ACKNOWLEDGMENTS

Thanks to Alessandro, Alberto, Chiara, Raffaella, Mana, Lena, Laura, and Mark, for reading this story and providing amazing feedback.

You were right. Wei isn't dead. This story proves it.

ACKNOWLEDGMENTS

ABOUT THE AUTHOR

I am an independent author living in Rome, the Eternal City. I grew up writing of falling empires, space battles, mortal betrayals, monumental decisions, and everything in between.

I wrote and published my first English book, *Lord of Time*, in between waiting tables and exploring the world.

I now spend my days traveling through time and space and, more often than not, writing about impossible but necessary worlds.

When I'm not busy chasing dragons or mastering the Force, you can find me at MicheleAmitrani.com or hanging out on Facebook at /MicheleAmitraniAuthor.